ICE

GALAXY ALIEN MAIL ORDER BRIDES: A QURILIXEN WORLD NOVELLA

MICHELLE M. PILLOW

MICHELLE M. PILLOW® - MICHELLEPILLOW.COM

ABOUT THE BOOK

ICE

She's hot. She's sexy. She's everything a lonely alien could want... except for the part where she captures him and puts him in a cage.

Alpha male alien Izotz (aka Ice Storm Chaos) isn't one for space exploration. He finds enough action fighting for survival on his frozen tundra of a home world. When the promises of Galaxy Alien Mail Order Brides tempt his brothers into signing up for a trip to Earth, he's hard-pressed to say no to the fantasy. Not many remain on the planet of Sintaz, and this may be his only chance to find a mate to warm the freezing nights. What he hadn't planned on was the fact the woman of his dreams would want to capture him and put him in a cage.

When Elle took the mercenary job hunting UFOs, she thought it would be an easy paycheck from an eccentric, crazy man. Little did she know extraterrestrials were real and freaking sexy to boot. If she can ignore the blue skin, surely this hunky alien can overlook the fact she's the reason he's now her boss' science experiment.

The Playful Prince
The Bound Prince
The Rogue Prince
The Pirate Prince

Captured by a Dragon-Shifter Series

Determined Prince

Rebellious Prince

Stranded with the Cajun

Hunted by the Dragon

Mischievous Prince

Headstrong Prince

Space Lords Series

His Frost Maiden

His Fire Maiden

His Metal Maiden

His Earth Maiden

His Woodland Maiden

Dynasty Lords Series
Seduction of the Phoenix
Temptation of the Butterfly

To learn more about the Qurilixen World series of
books and to stay up to date on the latest book list
visit www.MichellePillow.com

Dear Readers,

For those of you familiar with my bestselling series, Dragon Lords, you've already been introduced to the Galaxy Brides Corporation and the services they offer lonely men and women of the future. What you might not have known is that Galaxy Brides (formerly aka "Galaxy Alien Mail Order Brides") dabbled in taking grooms to destinations—namely Earth! Unfortunately, they found the alien males a little too hard to control once they landed on our surface.

I hope you have as much fun reading this series as I've had writing it!

Happy Reading!

Michelle M. Pillow

To the Pillow Fighter Fan Group
A big thanks to dedicated readers like you willing
to help spread the word about the books they love.
Thank you!

PROLOGUE

Planet of Sintaz

"Women."

Izotz remembered precisely three times when his youngest brother had a great idea. One, jumping off snow cliffs into the drifts below to avoid being eaten by a hungry bearguar. Two, giving unauthorized permission to the spaceship full of Galaxy Playmates to land on their ice-covered planet. Now *that* was how a man heated up the wintery nights on Sintaz. Three, traveling north to avoid an unpredictable ice storm.

This new idea? It didn't make the list. Not even close.

"Women," Edur repeated as if saying the word in an excited tone would make the idea better. It didn't.

"No," Izotz stated, his tone final. He was the oldest, and it was his responsibility to look after the other two.

"But, *women*," Edur persisted.

"He has a point," Tushar chimed in, supporting our youngest sibling. "Women."

"Do you even know where this *Erd* is?" Izotz asked.

Tushar gestured that he did not. "I think it's called *Arth*."

"And it has women," Edur added.

"Our mother should have dropped you in a snowdrift as a baby and left your blue ass there." Izotz tried to turn back to his meal. Things tended not to stay warm for long and already his broth was the temperature of the outside.

Well, maybe that was a little dramatic. Outside the broth would have been frozen solid.

"You could have been raised by a bearguar or a hairy bellaphant," Tushar added, also teasing

Edur, "walking around on all fours and roaring for your supper."

"*Rawr*," Edur roared. Only to add gruffly, "*Women.*"

Tushar bit back his laughter.

Izotz sighed in resignation. "You're not going to stop until I agree to listen, are you?"

"No," Edur and Tushar answered in unison.

"Fine. Show me the hologram." Izotz crossed his arms over his chest as he balanced on the stool. It had been built to his taller height so his feet could comfortably touch the floor. Their Sintazian home had three of almost everything—three stools, three eating utensils, three bowls, three beds. They didn't need anything else. After their parents had met with an ice storm while hunting, it was just the three of them.

Edur lifted his hand from beneath the eating platform sticking out of the wall and set a holographic chip on the surface, proving he had been holding it the entire time. He activated it.

The transparent image of a strange blue and brown planet swirling with white appeared in rotation as if it hovered over Izotz's food. He automatically pushed his bowl aside even though the hologram would not contaminate it.

"Is yours one of the many stagnant civilizations without enough women to produce offspring? Do you come from a monogamist culture with no one to marry? Or a polygamist culture in need of more food makers? Are you lonely and looking to reassign your assets? What if we told you there is a planet whose name is called Earth that could solution all your needs? Would you be jolly?" The deep male voice asking the questions was clearly a computerized translator and not a very good one at that. Foreign words from the original recording could be heard low in the background.

"Yes," Edur answered needlessly.

"Earth," Tushar said. "That's what it is called."

"Let me guess," Izotz muttered sarcastically, unimpressed with the sales pitch. "It has women."

"Earth has women they are willing to share," the male voice said.

Izotz smirked. "This translation is horrible, or the Earth people have awful grammar. Solution our needs? Earth is a planet, so it would be *it is* not *they are*, and—"

"Shh, just listen," Edur wave his hand for Izotz to be quiet.

"So, join us for jolly-making on Earth, where all your humanoid female fantasies can become digestible food."

Izotz reached to pause the recording. "No. I've heard enough. I'm not eating females."

"You know what the translator means." Edur frowned. He was right. Izotz knew that not many people spoke the Sintazian language, so the translators were often comically wrong. Though, it was usually enough to get the gist of what was being relayed. "It's not a food service. It's a bridal service."

Edur pressed the button to resume the recording.

"Earth has a breathable sky, food you can put in your heart, and..." The translator began speaking in an alien language as if the words could not be translated.

"Don't worry, it stops that in a second," Edur assured him.

"I wasn't worried." Izotz reached for his food. The fact it was cold put him in a grumpier mood.

"...officially discovered life forms not of their own planet but are humanoid compactible and ready for travel to their new homes," the translation continued.

"Compactible?" Tushar frowned, his demeanor changing. "They squish down?"

"Wait, a detailed image scan is coming up." Edur's excitement didn't die amongst the doubts of his brothers.

"Upon mate selection, all necessary papers will be given to the Earth government and transport will be taken upon us, as you leave the planet with your new—"

"Digestible food," Izotz said over the translator. Tushar laughed.

"Those wishing to stay on Earth will be provided with manly identity."

Izotz again turned off the translator. "No."

"You haven't seen their pictures," Edur insisted.

"I don't need to. Why would we leave?" Izotz asked. "We have everything we need. This is our home."

Edur stood and walked to the entry of their ice hut. He grabbed both handles and pulled the two doors open to reveal the barren landscape of snowdrifts and ice cliffs. He gestured his arms at the vast stretch of nothingness.

"That is the only reasonable argument you have made," Izotz said.

Edur shut the doors.

They were isolated, three of the very few who remained on the frozen globe of their home world. Many of the settlers had left with the ESC scientists who came to survey the landscape. For some reason, the alien organization wanted to set up base and start a hundred-year-long project mining fifteen-thousand feet below the planet's surface to test mineral compounds. Most of that time would be spent going through thousands of years of compacted snow, ice, and whatever else happened to have crashed on the planet to be forgotten. Rumor had it alien spaceships were buried all over the place. Those who hadn't hitched a ride with the ESC had found work on cargo ships hauling cold storage.

"Option one." The translator began speaking again. Tushar had turned it on.

Izotz glanced at the image of a humanoid woman. She stood, arms to her sides, rotating in a slow circle. Her clothing fit tight to her body and her brown hair fell long down her back.

"They're tinted strangely," Tushar observed, noting the non-blue of their flesh.

"Option two." Another woman replaced the

first image. This one had lighter hair, which grew high over her head. Her gown sparkled.

"At least they have the right number of limbs," Izotz said.

"Option three." The third woman held a rectangular object in her hands and wore black-rimmed eye protectors. She opened the rectangle to show alien words written inside. Her lips moved slightly as she read. "Option four." This time it showed a redhead in tight black clothing with smoke coming from her lips. "Option five." The woman wore two strips of clothing, over her chest and hips.

"Three," Izotz said. As more options appeared, the image of that woman stayed with him. "I will order option three."

Edur laughed. "I knew you would change your mind."

"I want five," Tushar said. "And two."

"Don't be greedy," Izotz scolded. "Take option two. Five will never survive our weather in her traditional garb."

"Fine. I'll take option two," Tushar muttered, clearly not happy with having to choose only one wife.

"You have our orders," Izotz told Edur. "Let

the aliens know to deliver them here. There is too much to be done for us to leave."

"It doesn't work like that. I think these are merely examples of what we will find when we go to the planet. They don't bring them here," Edur said. "We have to meet the women on their home world."

"It would be more convenient if they delivered brides to those seeking them." Izotz sighed. "Fine. We will take this trip to *Erd*—"

"Earth," Tushar corrected.

"—if we get the hunting done for the winter storms. We will need extra food supplies if we are to accommodate a larger family, and I imagine we will have to teach these women how to hunt our territories before they can help provide. We will also have to scavenge building materials to expand our home for when they come here to live with us."

"I'll arrange our travel." Edur grabbed the holographic device and hurried from the room.

"He didn't hear anything I said, did he?" Izotz shook his head and looked at the cold contents in his bowl.

"All he heard was yes," Tushar grabbed the bowl and took it toward the cook fire. He dumped the contents back into the kettle before pouring out a new serving. Nothing was wasted on Sintaz. It couldn't be. Food was hard to come by on an icy tundra. He set the rewarmed meal before his brother. "Do not look so worried. Space travel is safe, and they would not take us to Earth if there were anything to worry about. Companies like this wouldn't be in business if they lost customers on alien worlds. Think of it as a vacation."

"What is this company called, anyway?" Izotz turned his full attention to the meal.

"No idea," Tushar said. "But I trust Edur to suggest the most reputable."

2

I TRUST EDUR TO SUGGEST THE MOST reputable.

Izotz dove onto the alien ground, sliding over the dark surface. It was not slick like ice and bits of debris dug into his naked chest, scraping and stabbing his skin. A blast sounded, whizzing over him with a zap of electricity.

If this was how Earth people said hello, he hated to see what they were like angry.

From the first moment the Galaxy Alien Mail Order Brides corporation landed on Sintaz to pick up the brothers, the company had gone above and beyond to show their incompetence. They promised to join hearts across the universes by introducing men and women for mating purposes.

What they delivered was the wrong language uploads, slips of green paper Izotz and his brothers were supposed to believe acted as actual currency, and questionable Earth identification packages—seriously, he now had the Earth name of Ice Storm Chaos. Edur was Frost Chaos and Tushar was Snow Chaos.

Ice, Frost, and Snow? They might be considered popular, strong Earth names, but Ice had his doubts. Though, they did assure them that Spark, Flame, and Blaze from the fire planet of Bravon had been quite successful with their element-related names. Ice had begun to doubt those were even real alien clients.

Thankfully, the crew had managed to find them an upload for the Earth language, but only after he had been made proficient in Venimice. Like Ice needed to gurgle-speak to that nuisance race. Uploading data files into the brain might be a quick way of learning, but it left him with a headache. He didn't appreciate the unnecessary transfer. Now his thoughts were a jumbled mess of Earth English, Sintazian, and throat gurgles.

At least the spaceship hadn't stalled in the deep black and imploded. That was about the best thing he could say about the bumpy trip across the universes.

I trust Edur to suggest the most reputable.

Ice trusted his little brother to be thinking with the wrong set of brains. No... Little head? Was that the Earth saying? Thinking with a little head? That made no sense. Did Earth males have two heads?

Damn those uploads. They were distracting him as they dispersed themselves into his brain. Now was not the time to think of humanoid anatomy.

Another blast sounded. So much for Earth being a welcoming place to meet women.

Ice glanced up to see his brothers disappearing into the nearby trees. They had not realized he'd stayed behind to distract the alien enemy. Five attackers had come into the small clearing, cloaked in black and hiding in the shadows, as if they'd known where the spacecraft would land.

The strange coloring of his hands in moonlight caused him to do a double take. He would never get used to seeing the dark human-like flesh in place of his blue. Whatever pills they had given them to blend in were working. The fact they had to hide their identities probably should have been their first clue that Galaxy Brides might not have the permission to land that they'd claimed.

Ice rolled onto his back, ready to battle the Earthlings who attacked. A blaster hovered near his face and he jerked to the side, sweeping his arm up to knock the weapon away.

A low gasp sounded, but he could not see the person's face as a mask covered all but dark brown eyes. Those eyes kept him from striking a second time, more than restraints ever could. Had the Galaxy Bride people done something to him, something to stop him from harming an Earthling?

Logic told him to punch. Instead, he merely blocked the downward reach and rolled to the side.

The loud clank and slide of metal announced the closing of the Galaxy Brides' ship. They were leaving them here, unaided, with the attackers. Either the bridal corporation was incompetent, or this was a setup.

I trust Frost to suggest the most reputable.

"They went into the woods," a man yelled, running after Frost and Snow. "Spread out. Find them. Don't let them get away."

The brown-eyed Earthling recovered from

Ice's defensive move and tried to grab him. Ice pushed to his feet and seized the attacker's arm. He should have been able to stop the assault, but the creature was too nimble, and he was unable to stop the alien physically.

Curses on Galaxy Brides.

Ice tried to defend himself and push the alien away, without doing harm. However, when another human came at him, evidently thinking he didn't know how to spar, Ice had no problem launching that one into the air. He grabbed hold of a thigh and used the momentum of the man's attack to heave him on toward the others. The flailing human made contact with the backs of two of his brothers' pursuers and all three tumbled onto the ground. At their cries, the fifth gave up his pursuit and returned to fight Ice.

The momentary relief he felt at knowing his brothers were safe for the time being was short lived as he realized he was now alone on this strange orb. The sound of thrusters drawing power in preparation of a launch drowned out the human shouts. If that ship finished takeoff, they would be trapped on Earth with no way to get home.

This was a nightmare.

"Hey!" Ice yelled. He picked up a rock and hurled it at the ship, hoping to set off the sensors. He grabbed another, and then another, causing them to reverberate off the metal side.

Maybe they didn't realize.

Maybe they didn't know.

Maybe they had set the brothers up.

Curses on Galaxy Brides!

Four of the attackers were coming back for him. The fifth lay on the ground.

Ice picked up another rock, this time chucking it at the nearest figure. The stone hit its target in the shoulder, knocking the Earthling onto his back. The human made a strange noise. He did it again, this time striking a covered face. Before Ice could pick another rock, the two remaining humans charged, hands swinging. Curled fingers balled into complete fists. It was a strange way to fight.

As he lifted his outstretched hand to shove the heel of his palm into a face, he saw those brown eyes...and hesitated. Instead, he went for the other target. He landed a blow on a hard chest. The alien creature made an odd choking noise as he fell back.

He should have been able to take the last

attacker. He'd fought bearguars bigger than this human, but as he watched it pull the mask off its head, he realized the attacker was a woman.

She took a deep breath but did not run.

Ice stared at her mouth, waiting for her to speak. She circled him, her arms raised.

"*Guuuurgh-gurg,*" he said.

She stopped moving, her eyes widening by small degrees.

Ice frowned. *Stupid Venimice uploads!*

Before he could lift his arms, the woman had hold of them and was flipping him into the air. He flailed, landing on his back on the hard ground. The breath was knocked from his lungs, followed by an electric shock that reverberated through his body.

"*Gurgha,*" he mumbled, seconds before passing out.

3

Elle tapped her fingers against the reinforced glass observation window that overlooked the room in which they kept the alien male. Her forehead pressed against it as she watched him. Ice-blue eyes met hers, but he didn't move. In fact, he hadn't moved in three weeks. Not really. The striking color caused her to shiver. It's what had made her hesitate in her first attempt to stop him. She had wanted to be the one to take him down. The others would not have been so gentle. Even now her co-workers hunted the other two.

Though she would never say it out loud, she hoped they didn't find them.

There were times she hated her job. This was one of them.

The alien wore the white tunic and scrub pants of the facility. Whatever he'd taken to blend in was beginning to wear off and with each passing day, his skin turned from a darker brown to blue with patches that formed a tribal pattern on his arm. If she hadn't seen it for herself, she wouldn't have believed it.

Secret alien facility with an actual secret alien prisoner.

She was an alien mercenary. Her unofficial job title was actually a real thing. Go figure.

When she'd signed on for the job, she'd honestly thought it would be an easy paycheck from an eccentric, rich asshole who would send them on wild goose chases. She never thought they would catch something.

Correction, *someone*. These were living humanoid creatures. They were not things. They were people...kind of.

If she had known, Elle would never have agreed to this.

She moved along the glass, watching as his eyes followed her. At least there were still signs of life in those depths. She wished she could say something, communicate, find a way to judge his thoughts and his intent. Did he mean them harm? Was he seeking asylum? Why did his ship leave without him?

She wanted to tell him she was sorry.

Elle glanced along the white hall, listening for others. There was no one. The cameras were pointed inward at the alien, and they could not see where she stood along the edge of the glass. She placed her hand against the barrier, spreading her fingers as she gazed into his eyes. Alien facial expressions could not be expected to mimic human ones. His smiles might not mean happy. His frowns might mean joy. His black hair might be sensitive to the touch like tiny tentacles. He could have four separate hearts located in his limbs.

Well, okay, she knew that he had two hearts, the main organ and what looked to be an accessory organ located in the general vicinity of his chest. The scientists had scanned him while he was passed out upon intake and Elle had sneaked a look at the data.

Her eyes traveled lower to his stomach. The scans had not shown everything. He'd started to wake up, and they'd moved him into containment.

There was no telling how human this alien really was.

Okay, seriously, am I mentally undressing the extraterrestrial?

The thought was supposed to be self-scolding, but it had the opposite effect. It made her more curious to see what he looked like naked. She had not been there when they'd changed him, and she couldn't exactly ask Dr. Hanklen if the large alien came fully intact. With her luck, they'd get the idea to test out the full extent of his compatibilities with one of the two females in the facility—the rage-filled Dr. Petals or Elle. She doubted they'd send Dr. Petals in to seduce him. The woman had a permanent expression like she'd just ate a sour pickle.

As much as she mentally condemned herself, her body had a completely different reaction. It was interested in playing out this line of fantasy. What would happen if they threw her into the prison with him, vulnerable except for her own strength? Or tied her down so she couldn't fight Mr. Blue's advances? Would his looks be lusty? Would they be curious?

Her eyes went to his blue hands. They were

large, five-fingered, but with dark nails. How would they look against her skin?

Elle's breathing deepened, and she became acutely aware of her breasts as she leaned into the glass. She had seen his strength as he threw Larson like he didn't weight nearly two hundred pounds. She needed to get out of the facility. It was clear she'd been cooped up too long if she was fantasizing about the alien.

There was something unexplained about him that called to her. Maybe it was his eyes, the soulful dark gaze that seemed so lost and sad. She knew what it was like to feel alone. Her adoptive parents had been awesome. They loved her and gave her a good home, but she wasn't like them. There was still a part of her that wondered what life would have been like if her birth parents lived.

Her father was a hardworking man. Her mother was a homemaker who liked hosting dinner parties and fundraisers. Elle had another kind of drive. As an angsty teenager she'd found boxing, of all things. Somehow punching released all the pent-up emotions she carried inside. Then she found kickboxing. Then martial arts. Then survivalist training, which is what her somewhat boyfriend at the time called preparing for the end of times. She had thought it was Jimmy's ridiculous conspiracy theory hobby until he bought her a fake ID package for her birthday—well, her "new" birthday—complete with a birth certificate, social security card, and licenses. After that, she tried to avoid him and he technically broke up with her when he found a woman with a bug out shelter and apocalypse supplies. He'd been very sorry.

Then the Milano Foundation found her, and for some reason, she found herself telling them her name was Ellen Sharp, instead of her real name Elenore Rollins. Strangely, under both her real and fake identifications, everyone shortened her name to Elle. Except for some of the mercenaries she worked with. They called her Sharp. She had to give it to Jimmy. Whoever made the fake ID was good. It stood up to scrutiny.

Only, what amused her at first ended up isolating her. No one she worked with knew about the real her. They thought she was Ellen, a woman with no family, the perfect employee because she had no ties to distract her. In many ways, she felt like an alien among the others in the facility.

Her eyes again strayed down the alien's body.

She took a deep breath.

Fuck. She needed to get out of this stupid facility. Cabin fever was driving her to insanity.

Just as she was about to pull away and hide in her quarters, the alien moved.

She gasped, holding her breath as he stood. She glanced around, wondering if anyone was at the monitors to see what was happening. She kept her hand on the glass, not moving as she watched him step toward her.

His movements were slow, and her lungs began to burn as she waited to see what he would do. She forced herself to breathe. Those piercing eyes held hers and she couldn't look away, couldn't yell for help...not that she would.

"Hi," she tried to speak, but her lips barely moved and no sound came out.

He stopped before her, towering over her five-foot-five height.

The glass had become warm from the heat of her hand. The alien tilted his head slightly forward. The backs of his fingers swept up against the glass and rested near where her breasts had been. She found herself mesmerized, leaning forward, wondering what he would do.

Could he read her thoughts? Had he known what she'd been thinking about?

The idea should have caused embarrassment, but instead she found her body reacting favorably.

She wanted him. For as wrong, crazy, and ill-advised as that realization was, she wanted him.

Elle pressed harder against the glass, squishing her breasts in her need to be closer to him. She wanted to see what he would do. She wanted to know if he wanted her. Would they even be compatible? She wanted to find out.

"Do something," she whispered, her lips barely moving.

The backs of his fingers rested next to her right nipple—so close and yet she couldn't feel the touch.

Her eyes dipped to his mouth. Would he even know what a kiss was?

A loud bang sent vibrations over the glass as the alien struck the barrier. It was hard enough that it reverberated through her chest.

She jumped back.

He hit the glass again as if testing it.

Elle glanced over the empty hall and lifted her hands, gesturing that he should be quiet. "You don't want to do that."

He stuck the glass harder, leading with the heel of his hand.

"It's reinforced bulletproof—"

He hit so hard that a crack spider-webbed out from his hand.

Elle pressed her back against the hallway wall opposite the window. "Please, stop!"

He shouted something at her, the muffled words barely coming through the glass. What she could hear were strange gurgling noises.

"Shh." She motioned her hands frantically, willing him to quiet down.

The sound of running footsteps echoed down the hall. The others were coming. It was too late.

Larson appeared seconds before Dr. Hanklen and a couple of lab techs she didn't know the names of. Larson was a big, hulking brute of a man who didn't say much. It was a quality Elle appreciated in him.

In contrast, Hanklen wouldn't stop talking. No one ever did anything right, everyone else was always wrong, and he was the smartest man in the room...just ask him, he'd tell you. He was probably the reason Dr. Petals was angry all the time. Elle avoided the man whenever she could.

"What's happening? What did you do,

Sharp?" Hanklen demanded of Elle before shoving her out of the way. She stumbled but resisted the urge to shove back even if she could take the scientist easily in a physical fight.

The alien hit the glass harder, trying to expand the crack he'd made.

"Larson, get the subject restrained."

"Fuck, he's strong," Larson observed.

"Now!" Hanklen ordered. "Do what you have to, but I want him alive."

Larson rushed down the hall, turning the corner that would lead to the only door into the cell.

Elle tried to go after him, but Hanklen lifted his hand with a glare of warning.

"I can help. I didn't do anything," Elle said. She wanted to make sure they didn't hurt the captured man. "You need everyone—"

"Stay where you are, or I will have you escorted off the premises," Hanklen warned.

Elle began to move anyway. It wasn't in her nature to stand by.

Hanklen grabbed her arm. She swung around, her fist balling before she had the presence of mind to stop herself. If she punched the cagey doctor that would be assault. And he was just the kind of asshole who would find a way to press charges...or, come to think of it, he'd lock her up in the cell next to their blue prisoner. This facility tended to police itself, and he wouldn't want anyone getting word of what they did here.

Oh, but she wanted to hit the smug little man.

"Look!" A strange smile worked its way onto the doctor's face.

Elle turned to the alien. He was staring at them.

Hanklen kept hold of her arm, dragging her a few feet down the hall. "Look at his eyes. He's watching you. I think he likes you."

"You're delusional," Elle dismissed. The fantasy that had played out in her head was all too recent. That didn't mean the doctor wouldn't get some kind of idea. It's not like they were under the burden of government regulations. "He was slamming at the glass to get to me. He probably wants me dead. I did capture him, after all."

The disappointment on the doctor's face was palpable.

Larson pushed through the door to the cell, leading a group of amped-up men behind him.

Panic filled her, and it took all her energy to maintain her composure. She knew what was coming. There was no way the prisoner would win this fight.

And the fact he was here was her fault. She was the one who'd brought him to the facility. What happened next would be on her.

The alien's eyes met hers, and she did the only thing she could.

She mouthed, "I'm sorry."

"Excellent," Hanklen whispered, more to himself than her. "We can observe how the creature fights." His smile worried Elle.

4

WHY WAS THE PRETTY EARTH HUMAN taunting him?

Every day, she came to look at him, staring at him with those brown eyes that mesmerized him into losing the fight against her. She was the reason he was caught in this trap. And she came, every damned day, to look in on him like he was a pet.

Oh, but today had been different. Today, she had looked at him with narrowed eyes and flushed skin. His Galaxy Brides uploads had finally unpacked themselves into his brain, and he knew what seduction meant, knew what deepened breath, pinked cheeks, and pursed lips were an invitation to. Which could only mean she mocked him.

But, fuck, he wanted her. When she pressed her chest to the glass, he wanted to explore these things Earthlings called breasts. Sintazians didn't have soft globes like that. Their women were hard and muscled. This woman, though she would hold her own against any creature in battle, had softer edges. Curves even.

She made his body vibrate.

Many emotions flooded him as he spent time in the cell. What did they want with him? He'd heard about alien experimentation done by some species. Galaxy Brides had assured them Earth people were not like that.

Galaxy Brides had said a lot of things.

Galaxy Brides clearly could not be trusted.

Did these humans have his brothers? Were Snow and Frost safe? That fear was the most unbearable. He could handle a threat to himself, but his family? He wasn't sure what to do, so he kept himself very still to lull them into thinking he was docile. He watched them, counted them, looked for any sign of escape. Yet, they merely kept him in this room like an animal. Occasionally, they plunged devices into him to pull out his fluids. Blood, they called it here. And they gave him a strange, pasty substance for food that did not have much taste. The guard had called it oatmeal, and each time he ate they watched him as if waiting for something strange to happen.

Rage had filled him as the woman tried to arouse him. He'd been unable to contain himself as he struck the glass wall. He knew it was a mistake each time he struck, and yet...

The sound of the door crashing open interrupted his fast stream of thoughts. He turned, ready for battle. Better to go down fighting than remain trapped in this tiny room with only a bed and toilet.

Ice didn't think. He hated being afraid and alone and knew the only thing left was to fight his way out. The first man who charged him had murder in his eyes, all that hate directed at Ice. The feeling was mutual. Ice returned the hateful sentiment as he absorbed the man's punch to the face. He instantly swept his arm to the side, forcing the man upward so that he struck the glass. The broken rings Ice created had weakened the structure, and the force of the man's body finished the job.

The Earthling almost hit the seductress and

the little man holding on to her. They both scrambled out of the way. Neither of them extended an arm to their fallen comrade as they turned back to watch.

The woman's lips moved, but no sound came out. He wondered what it was she was doing. Did Earthlings have magic and spells? He knew the words, so they had to be actual things here, but the information was unclear.

He didn't have time to contemplate as he fought the Earth words flooding his brain. They were like a virus trying to take over his thoughts. There were times he had to force himself to think with the Sintazian language instead. Each time, he clung to a tiny piece of home.

Frustration and fear drove his actions. Even as he knew there were too many of them that didn't mean he wouldn't try. He punched, kick, threw, even headbutted those who entered the cell. Their warm bodies were merely targets, and their shouts were drowned by the smack of fists and feet.

Though it didn't surprise him, the end of the battle came too fast for his liking. He felt the familiar bite into his flesh, pumping the electrical current into him. Maybe this was magic, the way the device made him lose all function in his limbs.

He tried to resist, but the current forced him to his knees and then onto his back. With that, his small victories came to an end.

His eyes met the woman's through the broken glass. Those taunting brown eyes didn't appear happy, and yet she did nothing to aide him. The last thing to go was his eyesight, but the current took that from him too as his world went dark.

5

ELLE HELD IN HER MIND THE IMAGE OF THE
scientists ordering the mercenaries to haul the
alien from the damaged cell to another holding
facility. They acted as if he were no more than a
tranquilized rhinoceros to be carted on a floor
dolly from one place to another. Their laughter
echoed in her head. They thought it was funny—
the alien fighting for his life. They posed with the
unmoving body—pretending to hold the alien
down, grasping his hands in the air like they were
buddies, shooting thumbs-up as they snapped
photos on their phones—despite knowing those
phones would be confiscated before they left the
facility.

This was a game to them. In the eyes of the facility, this alien man was no more than livestock to be hauled from one pen to another.

And Elle had helped put him there.

How was she to know aliens were real? This was supposed to be a cushy job that sent her on fruitless chases around the world for an insane amount of pay. Hell, she'd even daydreamed through the "training" videos they'd shown her, and only recently had she read the full protocol manual—and that was only out of boredom.

Though he didn't communicate, she instinctively knew there was something more behind his eyes. He was not an animal. This was an intelligent being—and he needed her help.

Elle clutched Hanklen's keycard in her hand. This might be the biggest mistake of her life, one that would not only get her fired but would piss off some very powerful people. It's not like you could tell your millionaire boss to shove it where the sun doesn't shine without a little retaliation in return. Franky "The Heart Attack" Milano wasn't exactly the forgive-and-forget type.

Then there was the fact she was working off her impressions of this alien man, not actual facts.

She could be projecting herself and ignoring evidence. Facts were: he was an alien, he'd shown great strength and the ability to fight, she knew nothing about him or his people, and—most importantly—*he was a freaking alien.*

"I've lost it. I'm a mental case. If I do this, there is no turning back. I'll lose my job. I could be sued for breach of contract. Maybe not since they'd be looking for Ellen Sharp. The alien could suck my face off and eat my insides."

Even as she whispered the words to herself, Elle kept her fast pace. She tried to stay low as she moved down the hall passed laboratory doors with small windows. Her feet barely made a sound. She paused to listen before glancing around a corner and continuing.

The way she saw it, there wasn't a choice. She wouldn't be able to live with herself if she didn't try to help. Rounding up innocent people who hadn't done anything wrong was not something she wanted on her life resume.

Or maybe she really was having a mental breakdown.

Good money would bet on the breakdown.

Elle slipped the keycard into her back pocket

before turning the corner to the guarded cell. She pursed her lips, feigning annoyance. Jim Berry guarded the cell door. He was an amiable man though a little slow on the uptake and only a mediocre fighter. But he was dependable. He always showed up on time and always brought the supplies he was told to. He was a man meant for taking orders.

Unlike last time, the alien was kept in a metal room with no windows. Even though it was supposed to be a temporary holding cell, they jokingly called it solitary confinement, and the term wasn't all that far off from the truth.

"Hey, Berry," Elle greeted, her tone flat. "How's he doing today? Any trouble?"

"Quiet as a church mouse," Berry answered. "Sorry I missed out on all the action. Figures the one time something interesting happens around here, I'm off duty and sleep through it."

"It was something," Elle agreed with a nod. "I'm betting in a few weeks you'll get your chance."

The man actually looked hopeful.

"But for now, I've been sent to relieve you of your post."

Berry's expression fell. "But I'm on duty for

another," he glanced at the watch on his wrist, "three hours."

"And I'm on shift for the next twenty." Elle smirked and gave a humorless laugh. "Apparently, they don't like it when you incite a prisoner, and he causes damage to company property. I just spent the last hour getting my ass handed to me by Hanklen. If I want to keep my job, I have to pay for the window out of my checks, and I'm on permanent guard duty until otherwise instructed."

"Whoa, that's rough," Berry swore.

Elle shrugged. "What can you do? Orders are orders."

"Did they say where they wanted me to report?" Berry looked hesitant to leave.

"Sounds like they're going to be making another run out tonight. If I were you, I'd go to the mess hall and grab something to eat while you have the chance." Elle leaned her back against the wall by the metal door and sighed. "Rumor has it they're doing a Southern theme today—biscuits and gravy, chicken, fried green tomatoes, fried okra, fried everything."

Berry nodded. "Want me to sneak you something?"

"Nah, I'm good, thanks. I'm going to take my punishment like a champ." Elle didn't move away from the wall as she yawned and looked up at the ceiling.

Berry left, walking much slower than she would have liked. Any other person would have run the second she'd said she was relieving them of boring guard duty. Berry would probably get to the mess hall and have his first bite of biscuits and gravy before getting worried and coming back to check that it was honestly all right for him to leave.

She needed to have the alien gone by then.

She waited a few seconds after he disappeared around the corner and prayed that she'd timed this right, when no one would be manning the security feed.

Elle grabbed the keycard from her pocket and pressed it to the door pad. The unit beeped, and she heard the metal door unlatching.

Elle took a deep breath and told herself, "This is the right thing to do."

She pushed the long handle down and pulled the heavy door. Her hands shook, and she held her breath. She didn't know what she would find.

Inside, the room was dim and had a musty

smell, like the stale air in a chest closed up for too long. She stepped in slowly. A tiny voice whispered in the back of her mind to slam the door and retreat. She ignored the fear. Yet, when she opened her mouth, no sound would come out.

It took a moment for her eyes to adjust to the light. The room was worse than she remembered. The bare stone walls and floor were cold and unwelcoming. There was no place to sit down. But there was a place to be chained up—and that's where she found him.

The alien was locked against the wall, held in place by rusted manacles. He hung limp, the metal biting into his skin as it held him up. Dark spots had formed on his face and naked chest as if he had been beaten while held in place. There were no cameras in this room, so she'd not been able to see what happened.

She shut the door, closing them in. Keys hung on the wall, and she grabbed them. "Are you awake?"

Ice blue eyes opened to look at her. They froze her in mid-action.

"Can you...?" She forced herself to stand before him. "Can you understand me?"

He continued to stare.

"Of course not. Why would you speak English?" She gave a derisive laugh.

The alien opened his mouth and made a gurgling noise as if he were being strangled.

"Shh, quiet. I'm not here to hurt you." She dared to touch his arm, and the noise stopped. His skin was cool to the touch. He jerked away from her fingers.

"You smell like fall," she whispered in awe. "Like spice cake and pinecones."

He didn't move, didn't signify he understood.

"Don't make me regret this, but..." She lifted the key slowly to the manacle on his arm. "But you don't understand a damn thing I'm saying, do you? That's okay. I'm not exactly sure how to start explaining things to you, anyway. I mean, you have no reason to trust me. I wouldn't if I were you. Though, I am sorry. I wish I could make you understand at least that much."

She slipped the key in and paused.

"Please don't hurt me." She turned the key in the lock. The manacle clicked open, releasing him.

Before she could blink, a hand was on her throat and she was pressed awkwardly against the wall. Cool flesh met her arm where they touched. She resisted the urge to fight.

"I'm trying to help you," she whispered. She lifted the hand holding the keys. "Please, let me help."

He moved his gaze to where she jingled the keys...and then slowly released her.

Elle took a shaky breath as she moved to unlatch his ankles, keeping an eye on him for movement. She glanced over her shoulder at the door before reaching to unlatch the last one. Her mouth felt dry, and she licked her lips. She pushed the key inside the lock. The latch opened, and she paused. Seconds ticked by before she lowered her hands.

"I—"

The word barely made it out of her mouth before he had her pinned to the stone wall again. His hands gripped her arms as he lifted her off the ground. His body turned, pinning her legs with the side of his thigh. Hard eyes bore into hers.

"I'm trying to help you," she said. "We don't have time for this. Please, this is the only chance I'll get. When they find out I stole the—"

The alien shifted his body and leaned his face closer.

She gasped, tensing, but instead of a headbutt—he kissed her.

The cold lips pressed to hers, and she stiffened in shock. His eyes didn't close, and hers stayed open wide. His lips didn't move, but they didn't have to. The intimate contact sent a shiver over her. An odd vibrating started along her body, and she jerked her lips away.

"Earthquake," she said in shock.

Only, it wasn't. The vibration was coming from him.

He studied her a moment before releasing her. Her legs were weak from the contact and she fell to the ground. The alien ran for the door before she could stop him. He flung it open.

"Wait!" Elle ordered, she surged to her feet and rushed after him, only to find him going the wrong way down the hall. He'd end up in the mess hall or the dorms where everyone slept. She grabbed his arm, pulling hard to get him to stop. When he looked at her, she gestured that he should follow her.

The alien hesitated as she backed away from him, continuing to circle her hand, indicating that he was to go with her.

Finally, he stepped after her, and she quickened her pace as she did her best to lead him to safety.

"Fuck, I'm an idiot," she said under her breath. Her heart beat wildly, and adrenaline pumped through her veins. "What am I doing? This is stupid. What am I doing? What am I...?"

6

Ice debated on whether he could trust her. This could be a game to see what he'd do. The woman had captured him, brought him here with the others, and now she helped him? It didn't make sense. Then again, nothing on this weird planet made sense.

Oh, how he missed the isolation of his frozen home world. To think he'd thought it a good idea to come here. He should never have agreed to this trip.

What else could he do though? He didn't know his way around the alien facility, and this woman was the only one who appeared to have any kindness in her. She held up her hand. He kept walking. She stepped in front of his path and pressed her palm hard to his chest before wrapping her hand over his mouth. She wanted him to be quiet. When he did as she indicated, she relaxed, pointed at her ear and then at the turn in the corridor.

He tilted his head, hearing footsteps. He tensed, lifting his arms to fight. She motioned at him and kept still. The sound grew fainter and was followed by a loud bang as if a door closed.

She nodded at him and leaned to look around the corner. Soon he found himself following her in a strange rhythm—run, stop, hide in a tiny room with many toilets, run, duck, pause, hide in a shelf-filled room with stacks of material, strange bottles and containers.

She grabbed black material from a shelf and thrust it at him. "Put this on."

He looked at it and then her.

"I can't do anything about your skin color, but I can try to hide you until we make it out of here." She took the material from him and unfolded it to reveal a shirt. She threaded her hands into the armholes before grabbing his. She pulled his arms through the holes. Then she finished dressing him by forcing the material over his head.

As the material remained bunched on his chest, not fully falling to his waist, she returned to the shelf and came back with pants. She hesitated as she looked at his waist. She reached for him as if she would pull the white pants from his hips. Her breathing deepened, and he thought about kissing her again.

Sure, it would be stupid, but he wasn't exactly thinking with...

Oh, so *that's* what the human words "thinking with your little head" meant. Now he understood the phrase.

Clever, clever humans.

She pulled his shirt down all the way and tugged on his waistband, leaving the pants he wore in place before handing him the black ones. He thought about pretending he didn't understand what she wanted him to do. But then, considering the circumstances, playing games right now wasn't the best of ideas.

He pulled the pants from his hips, kicking them aside.

She made a small noise, and he glanced up to see her eyes focused on the nearby shelf a little too hard, giving the metal rack more attention than it deserved.

Ice hid a smile as he dressed.

"I hope you know where to meet your ship because I don't have a clue where to take you," she said. "The men haven't been successful in finding the other aliens that you landed with, so hopefully they've made it home safely."

Ice felt relief in knowing his brothers weren't here. Though, he couldn't help but wonder if that was why she'd released him. Did they think to use his obvious attraction to her against him? Did she think he'd lead her to his family?

Either way, it didn't matter. As soon as he was free of this place, he would rid himself of the woman and find his family on his own—even if he had to search the entire planet.

She glanced at him and, seeing him dressed, took shoes off of a shelf. She leaned over to put them on his feet.

"You'll need this jacket and," she placed a cap on his head, "this."

When he didn't put on the jacket, she grabbed his arms and threaded them into the sleeves. Glancing over him, she nodded. They went to the door. She looked out—and suddenly pushed on his chest to make him back up before continuing out the door.

"Hey, Ken, they got you out patrolling the border?" her muffled words came through the door. He leaned his ear against it to better hear.

"What gave it away?" came a wry response.

"My bad," the woman quipped. "I should have known you wore desert camo to pick up drunk chicks at the local dive bar."

"Eat me, Elle," the man said.

"Not even if you were the last meal on Earth," she responded.

Moments ticked by before the door opened again. She grabbed his arm and pulled him out.

"Ugh, that Ken is a dick. You have my permission to melt him with eye laser beams or whatever you aliens do."

Ice couldn't melt anything with his eyes, but he made a mental note that this Ken man possibly deserved death.

"Damn, this would be easier if you spoke my lang—"

A blaring siren sounded, and red lights began to flash. The woman's demeanor changed instantly, going from stealthy to panicked.

"Keep your head down and we might just make it out of here." She grabbed his hand and forced him to run. It wasn't long before he heard others behind them.

"Lock it down. Lock it down!" a man yelled. "Sharp?"

"On it," Ice's liberator yelled.

"Sharp, stop," the man shouted back.

She ran faster.

"Sharp, that's an order!"

There were no more warnings. A loud pop sounded behind them seconds before a light fragmented over their heads. Tiny shards rained down as they ran under them.

Another shot sounded, this time striking the wall by Ice's shoulder.

She jerked around a corner. She lifted his hand and placed pieces of metal into his palm. "I hope you know how to use keys and drive. Look for the blue sedan by the number seven." She held up seven fingers then drew the number seven in the air before she pushed him away, indicating he should keep running. "You go. I'll hold them off as long as I can. Whatever you do, don't stop."

She turned her back on him, bracing herself as the footfalls came closer.

Ice frowned. He was not leaving her.

He spun her around and tossed her over his

shoulder before running full force in the direction she'd told him to go. The woman struggled in protest at his plan. Ice didn't care. If she truly was scared of these other Earthlings, he was not leaving her behind to face them alone. They would escape together.

The annoying siren kept blaring, cutting the sound of his running so that it came in punctuated bursts. Two large doors came into focus and he charged faster. More shots were fired, ricocheting around them. Something stung his leg and arm, but he kept going. He charged through the doors, leading with this palm to slam them open.

The dark room that greeted them smelled like the engine room of a spaceship.

The woman kicked. "Put me down!" He let her go, and she slipped off his shoulder. "*Fuck*, you can run." She hurried back to the door and took something out of her pocket. She slid it against the wall and began punching numbers into a keypad.

"Lockdown," a serene voice said. The beeping continued on the other side of the door. "In three, two, one, initiated."

Fists pounded as the men shouted at them

from the other side. "Sharp, goddamn it, open the door!"

She sighed heavily and gave a small smile. "That will hold them for a second. Come on."

She tugged his arm, taking him to a blue sedan by the number seven. He knew what a car was from the uploads, but he had never seen one. He looked at it curiously and continued to follow her.

"No." She stopped him. "Get in the passenger side."

He didn't know what that meant.

"Argh, come on," She grumbled, tugging him around the vehicle to the others side. She opened the door, placed her hand on his head, and roughly guided him to get in.

Ice watched her run around to the other side. She slid in next to him, jamming the metal keys into the dashboard and revving the engine to life. Within seconds, they were driving through the dark room, past lines of various-shaped cars.

She stopped, lowering her window to rub her magic card against a box. The wall lifted, streaming sunlight into the darkness. A golden landscape stretched before them, shaped like the icy tundras of home, and a wave of longing washed over him. Specks of color dotted the ground.

As they drove out into the sunlight, he felt the heat intensify on his skin and he uncomfortably drew his arm away from the direct ray of light into the shaded areas of the car's interior.

"Welcome to the Utah desert, blue man. Now let's get you the hell off this planet."

7

"Elenore Rollins, how far you have fallen," Elle mumbled as she reached her hand into the partly opened window and shoved her arm as far as it could go. Her fingers fished for the knob so she could unlock the door. Stealing a rundown, prairie-tan-colored 1997 Ford Thunderbird wasn't exactly on her bucket list of things to do, but here she was. It was the only car in the parking lot that had an open window—and a small screwdriver shoved into the ignition.

As the tips of her fingers touched the lock, she flicked them several times to get it unlatched. Her eyes met the alien's where she'd placed him in the shadows. The sun was setting, which was good, because it seemed to be having an adverse effect on him. Though he didn't speak, he'd spent most of his time staring at a bright dot of light on the dashboard, watching it move as she sped them away from the desert facility. It reflected off a laminated parking pass hanging from the mirror.

It would make sense. His core temperature seemed lower than a human's. He was cooler to the touch and probably did have adverse reactions to heat. The desert was conceivably the worst place possible for him. His skin color appeared adapted to the colder climate, or at least blue made her think cold. She wasn't a biologist, so she could just be pulling nonsense out of thin air.

The knob popped up, and she sighed in relief. After glancing around the parking lot, she waved the alien over. He walked toward her, his stride strong, as if he didn't realize the danger they were in. It was probably just as well. It would have been worse if he was acting sketchy and panicked.

"Ma'am, do you know that man?"

Elle was startled by the voice. She'd been staring at her travel companion and had stopped paying attention to her surroundings. It was a rookie move. She turned to the speaker, realizing she'd been frozen in place with her hand on the door handle.

"Ma'am?" The older gentleman had a slight Southern drawl to his words. He began to walk toward her when she didn't have a fast answer. It wouldn't look good, her not moving and a man coming at her from the shadows, all dressed in black.

"What? Oh, yeah, yeah, that's my boyfriend." Elle held up her hand along the small of her back, trying to communicate that he should stop. The alien's footsteps kept coming, boots crunching on pebble-littered asphalt.

"You do know he's covered in blue paint, don't ya, ma'am?" The man relaxed his stance, and he smiled. "Halloween isn't until next month."

She felt a hand on her shoulder and glanced at the blue fingers gripping her. The alien tried to pull her behind him. She placed her hand on his and resisted his efforts. "Costume party in the desert."

The Southerner nodded as if that made complete sense. "You two kids be safe."

"Thank you, we will." Elle waited a few seconds to make sure the man left before opening the door. To the alien, she said, "Get in."

He studied her face. His eyes moved as he

looked over her features. She remembered his kiss in the holding cell.

"We have to keep moving," Elle said. She reached for his head to guide him into the car. But as her fingers met with the strands of black, she hesitated. His hair was soft. There were so many similarities between them—noses, eyes, lips. It was enough to make her wonder at the strangeness of it all. How could an alien, from another planet, evolve to look so much like a human?

She hadn't been brave enough to watch him undress. She wasn't sure she wanted the answer to *that* particular question.

"How is it you...?"

She felt a tiny vibration in her fingertips.

"Aliens are supposed to be...different." She let her fingers move through the strands of hair. "Tentacles and giant heads with scary black eyes that reflect like mirrors and..." Elle took a deep breath. "Get in."

Elle pushed at his head, guiding him down and into the passenger seat. She shut the door and ran to the driver's side. She reached for the handle, realizing she'd not unlocked it.

Elle looked in the window and pointed toward the knob. She tapped the glass.

He looked at her finger and didn't move.

Sighing, she started to go back around. As she made it to the front of the car, she saw him lean over through the windshield. He flicked his finger on the knob, pulling it up.

Elle turned back around and opened the door.

"Thank you," she said as she slid into the seat and slammed the door shut. She turned the screwdriver key. The engine sputtered a little but did eventually start. "I had an old rust bucket like this once. Lucky for us, they probably leave the window cracked so they can break into their own car."

She glanced at the alien, but he didn't speak. No surprise there.

The smell of the vehicle became noticeably strong, and she turned to see old bags of fast food takeout and pizza boxes had been thrown into the backseat. "Figures. The one car I can manage to steal, and it hasn't been cleaned since the year it came out of the factory."

Still nothing.

Elle drove them out of the parking lot, well aware they were in a stolen vehicle. She'd left the keys in the sedan and the doors unlocked, hoping someone would take it and lead anyone looking for them on a wild goose chase.

When they made it to the edge of town, she was able to breathe a little easier. Feeling his eyes on her, she glanced to the side several times. He stared at her face, not looking around them at the darkening landscape.

"I can't very well go around introducing you as my boyfriend. What do they call you?" She didn't wait for an answer. "They call me Elle Sharp, but I'll let you in on a secret. My real name is Elle Rollins."

His eyes still stared at her.

Elle pointed at her chest. "Elle." She pointed at him expectantly before repeating the gesture. "Elle."

He glanced at her pointed finger.

"Fine. You look like a..." She tried to think of a good name but drew a blank. "You look like a freaking blue alien I helped escape from a secret lab."

"Ice."

"Yeah, you look like an ice—" Elle gasped, jerking the wheel in surprise as she realized what just happened. He'd made a noise! She righted the car before she ran them off the road. The alien braced his hand against the dash. "Did you say ice?"

"That is what you may call me." The words were clear, slightly accented but spoken in perfect English. "My Earth name. Ice Storm Chaos. That is what they call me, but I will also give you a secret. My real name is Izotz."

"You..." She gripped the wheel tight. He had understood *everything* she'd said to him. Her mind raced as she tried to remember all the rambling thoughts she'd said out loud as they'd escaped the facility. "You understood... You can speak... Wait, did you say you're named Ice Storm Chaos? Like some kind of wrestler or something? How—?"

"The Galaxy Alien Mail Order Brides' crewman gave me the name. I am from a planet filled with ice. There are storms. They said it was a strong Earth name that women would enjoy." He turned his eyes forward. "Are you to drive on the painted mark like that? That other vehicle does not seem to be doing the same."

She glanced forward. The car had drifted into the middle of the highway and she quickly pulled back onto her side of the road seconds before a pickup truck sped past.

Galaxy Alien Mail Order Brides?

Surely that was a mistranslation. That hardly felt like it could be a real thing. An alien matchmaking service? *That's* what their visit was all about? Alien guys were coming to Earth to find wives?

"And Chaos?" she asked.

"Frost chose the..." He took a deep breath.

"Surname?" she supplied, thinking he was having trouble thinking of the right word. "Last name?"

"Family indicator," he answered.

"Family?" Elle nodded, understanding. "Those other men are your family."

"I will go to them. You will take me." He nodded as if it was that easy.

"Are they your brothers?" she asked.

"Yes, we come from the same parents."

"Where are you from?" Elle tried to keep calm. It was one thing to be rescuing an alien from a cage like a liberated animal who could take minimal commands, and quite another to communicate fully with an intelligent life form from another planet.

She was *freaking* talking to a *freaking* outer space extraterrestrial alien man.

"Earth does not have a word, but the closest sound would be Sintaz."

She worked her fingers against the wheel. There were so many logical questions she should ask, but she had a hard time thinking of them.

"Wh-why did you pretend you couldn't understand what I was saying?" Another car passed, and she glanced up to watch the taillights in the rearview mirror.

"I did not understand why you were helping me. Now I do. You have chosen me to be your boyfriend."

The statement caused an unexpected burst of laughter. It was short-lived. He was serious. "I just told that guy you were, so he'd leave us alone."

"You made your intentions known. I accept." The words were matter-of-fact as he watched the road.

Elle was at a loss for words. Maybe he didn't understand what a boyfriend was. Maybe he thought he was male, and they were friends? It wasn't a topic she wanted to explore at the moment.

A combination of nerves and excitement filled her. There was something about this man that attracted her. It made no logical sense. It was not something she felt comfortable saying aloud to other people. Yet, no one was here to judge her.

"If you didn't know my intentions were to help you, why did you kiss me?" The second the intimate question was out of her mouth, she wanted to pull it back. Her mind did *not* need any help going down this avenue of thought.

Her eyes strayed to a dark turnoff leading down a country road. She stayed on the highway.

"Because you let me." His mouth shifted, and she could have sworn he smiled. Shadows crossed his face as they drove. "And you make my body vibrate."

Don't ask, Elle, don't ask.

"Vibrate?"

Shit, why did I ask?

"I mean," Elle said, "are you hungry? Do you need food? Do you need...water? Anything?"

"I am told my system is compatible with Earth food, except for berries. I am to avoid berries." He tugged at his sleeve, slipping his arm out of the jacket before grabbing the shoulders and pulling both the jacket and shirt over his head. He breathed deeply as if disrobing brought him some relief.

"I noticed you didn't like the sun when it

came through the window earlier." She tried to turn on the air conditioning on the consul, but it was no surprise it only blew warm air. She turned it off.

"It is not the sun," he said. "It is the heat. My body is not used to such extreme temperatures. These scratches do not help."

It was only about seventy degrees out. "What scratches?" She glanced over his naked chest. The muscle structure was close enough to pass for that of a human.

He turned in his seat and pointed at his arm. A deep cut sliced along the biceps.

"Were you hit when they fired at us?" She tried to grab his arm, but it was too far for her to reach and drive at the same time. "Why didn't you let me know?"

She couldn't believe she'd missed a bullet wound.

"They are scratches."

"They?"

He pointed at his leg, near the hip. "They will heal once my body is cooler. I am not concerned. When do we reach my brothers?"

"I'm not sure where they are. The good news is, they weren't captured. The bad news is, there is a whole lot of territory they could have gone to. I'm driving us toward Colorado. It's where some of the scouts tracked them to before they lost the trail." She tried not to stare, but it was difficult to keep her eyes on the road. "Do you know where they're heading?"

His expression changed by small degrees at the question. "We were supposed to be met by guides to take us to the place."

"Which place?"

"The place where we were going."

A sign for a gas station prompted her to look at the gauge. They were low on fuel. "We need to stop. I'll grab cash from the ATM, but we'll have to make it last. I hate to sound paranoid, but it wouldn't surprise me if they can track my cards."

His naked blue arm lifted, and he turned in the seat. "I liked the first transport better than this one."

She gave a small laugh. The breeze through the partly open window did little to help the smell. "It's like my mom always said, beggars can't be choosers."

"You do not look like a beggar, so you should be able to choose a different transport."

"You do understand that we stole this car,

don't you? We took something that doesn't belong to us. Yes, it was out of necessity, but it's still wrong. Some person is going to wake up tomorrow and be—"

"Joyful that they no longer have to be in this contraption?" he offered.

"This month is not turning out at all like I'd expected," she said, more to herself than to him. She turned the car off the highway toward the solitary light of the gas station. "I'm an unemployed car thief on the run with a wanted man."

"I am a Sintazian trapped on an alien planet by the company hired to help us, and I can't find my brothers," Ice stated. "I am not sure I will ever see the ice tundras of home again."

"You win," Elle answered.

"What do I win?"

Instead of explaining the nuances of Earth language, she said, "You'll need to put the jacket and hat on and try to stay out of sight while we're here. The fewer people who see you, the better."

8

Ice watched Elle insert a device into the side of the car. She held it there, waiting, not unlike the fuel dock worker refueling a spaceship. The distinct smell of a ship's engine room combined with the stench of the vehicle. This was not the kind of place he wanted his woman to be in.

Girlfriend. That was the pairing word to boyfriend. Elle was his girlfriend.

The thought gave him pleasure. He had thought her behavior strange at the facility when she came to watch him, pressing herself to the glass and taunting him, had been designed to torture him. How wrong he had been. It must be an Earth woman dating custom. She had been trying to pair with him.

Earth women decided fast, and without any of the formal, traditional Sintazian fighting and hunting rituals. Though, there was that brief fight when he'd first landed. That must have been when she'd made up her mind. This was probably why Galaxy Brides had been so confident in their abilities to find wives on this world.

Concern over Frost and Snow kept him from suggesting that she stop driving so they could further the Earth dating custom that Galaxy Brides had explained to him of eating in a restaurant which led to kissing, which led to mating. But such things would have to wait. As soon as he found his brothers, they'd find a way to go home. He couldn't wait to show Elle her new home.

The gas station was not busy. A car was parked by the wide glass doors. Another vehicle had been leaving as they'd pulled up. Elle disappeared from view and he got out of the car for a better angle. He still couldn't see her.

Without much thought, he shut the door and walked toward the windows. A car pulled into the lot. The woman driver stared at him, her face pursed as if he had personally offended her. In the back seat, two small humans laughed. One waved his hand in the air. Instead of stopping, the woman looped around the lot and kept going.

Ice continued toward the building. The doors jingled when he pushed them open. The noise caused the man behind the counter to glance up from a small box. It took Ice a moment to think of the word—television.

Two women—one with dark hair, one blonde—paused, their hands resting on a container filled with brightly colored sticks. The distinct smell of the fueling ports didn't continue into the building. Instead, there was the hint of cooking meat.

When the man and two women continued to stare, he said, "Costume party in the desert."

The man nodded a few times and then turned his eyes back to the television. The women laughed and glanced at each other.

"Trick or Treat," the blonde whispered.

"I wouldn't mind a trick if the treat looked like that," the other answered.

They again laughed. Ice didn't bother addressing them further.

"Elle," he stated. "Elle."

"Ice?" She appeared from an aisle. "I told you to wait in the car. What are you doing in here?"

"I could not see you through the glass." He glanced around, relieved that he could perceive no threat.

"Dude," the guy behind the counter said. He was staring at the television, shaking his head.

"I managed to get cash from the ATM," Elle said. "Pick out something to eat and we'll get on the road. I don't want to stay here too long."

He looked around. "I do not know what is food."

She gestured to the aisles. "All of this—chips, candy, nuts."

"Meat?"

"You want a hot dog? All right." She led the way down the aisle and stopped at a strange contraption that rolled meat tubes up and down a flat platform.

"Some fucking crackheads robbed Junior's Pharmacy near Denver," the man at the counter said, though it wasn't apparent who he talked to as he stared at the box. Snickering as if it was the funniest thing he'd ever witnessed, he continued, "They manage to get away and the pharmacist dude is all '*they were very polite for criminals robbing me,*' but they fucking took nothing but a few crates of baby aspirin, boxes of candy bars, but left the money in the register."

"Anything else?" Elle asked Ice.

"Baby aspirin," Ice stated.

"You do know that you can't get high off it..." She eyed his face. "I don't think."

"What is high?"

"Never mind. Is it the scratches? Are you in pain?"

"They will heal once I am colder."

"There are stronger medicines, though I don't know if they'll mess with your biology. They might be toxic. Are you sick?" Elle touched his forehead, and he jerked away in surprise.

"This does not seem like the place." Ice tried to stop his body's vibrations. It was difficult around her.

"The place to find baby aspirin?" She glanced around. "Hold on."

As Elle disappeared, he went toward the counter man. "Where is this Denver where the fucking crackheads are?"

The guy looked at him and smirked. "Are you serious, man? Denver? The capital of Colorado? Everyone knows Denver."

Colorado. That is where Elle said the men

had been hunting his brothers.

"Is it far?"

"Not very," the man said.

The idea brought Ice more hope than he had dared to feel for a while. His brothers were close.

"Got the baby aspirin." Elle slid a bottle on the counter before unburdening her arms of the other items she carried.

The counter man laughed and began scanning the items so that his machine beeped. "Good one. Better be careful. Someone might try to jack you in the parking lot."

"What is jack?" Ice asked, confused.

"Where did you find this one?" The counter man shook his head. He stuck the items in a bag and then lifted it.

"Spaceship," Elle quipped. She took the bag and smiled.

The man laughed. Elle's smile deepened. Ice frowned.

"Why would you tell him that?" Ice grabbed her arm, ready to run.

The man laughed harder. "I don't know what he's on, but I want some. Have fun at your desert rave."

Elle said something, but Ice was too busy

looking around to see if anyone was coming for them. She pushed at his back, moving him toward the door. He walked in front of her like a shield, keeping her from outside harm.

When they were on the sidewalk, she said, "I told him you were from space because he'd never think I was serious, and I needed to say something to lighten the mood. You looked as if you wanted to bite the man's head off."

"Ew." He recoiled at the thought. "Why does everyone keep trying to get us to eat people? I do not dine on humans. Though Galaxy Brides did say that was an option. I will not eat you."

She pressed her lips together as if suppressing laughter. "That's too bad. Guess I'll be making other plans for the night."

"You wish for me to eat you?"

"Come on, lover boy, let's go." She strode away from him toward the car. "We need to get on the road."

"I am a man, or a boyfriend, but not a boy," he stated.

"Just get in the car, Ice," she said.

He glanced around the parking lot to make sure there was no danger before obeying the command.

9

"Eat this." Elle handed Ice the hot dog before placing the bag on the floor near his feet. She started the car and drove them out of the parking lot. She'd bought a bag of crappy convenient store food, but she actually enjoyed it. "My dad calls this road trip food. It was the only time my mom let us eat junk when I was a kid. But since I'm an adult, I can eat junk whenever I want."

"Is junk not garbage?"

"Can be."

He held the hot dog out for her to take. She ignored his hand as she turned the wheel toward the highway. "I will not eat from the garbage."

"It's a figure of speech. You need to eat." She

gave him a side-eye look. "I assume you need to eat."

He lifted the hot dog to his nose and sniffed. Then, slowly opening his mouth, he brought the foil toward his lips.

"Whoa, stop." She placed her hand between his face and the food. His mouth hit the back of her hand, his teeth grazing her skin as he bit her. He recoiled from her hand.

"I told you I did not wish to eat you," he stated. "Do not try to put yourself in my mouth again."

"You have to take it out of the wrapper first." Elle snatched the hot dog from him and began steering with her knees as she tore the foil-lined paper. She gave it back to him before putting her hand on the top of the wheel, so she could see the damage his bite had caused. There was a distinct dotting of blood patterned across the back of her hand.

"I have soda, water, juice…" She reached down to feel for the bag while still keeping her eyes on the road. "I'd probably start with the water. Humans need to hydrate. I'm not sure what Sintazians need, but water seems the safest bet."

"This meat tastes..." He examined the bite he'd taken from the hot dog.

"I know, I'm sorry. They didn't have a lot of meat options." She felt the top of a bottle and pulled it into her lap. Hopefully the caffeine would help keep her awake for the long drive ahead.

"It is good." He nodded in approval. "I like your hot dogs."

"Okay, then great." She screwed the lid off the soda. "The baby aspirin is in the bag if you still have a headache."

He took another bite and glanced toward his feet. He dug into the bag and pulled out the bottle. He shook it a few times. "The aspirin is inside the wrapper?"

She nodded. "It is."

He tore the box open and then looked around before throwing it in the backseat with the rest of the trash. He fumbled with the child safety lid, trying to pry it with his fingers. She took it from him, turned it so that the notches lined up, and then popped it open.

He took it from her, sniffed it, and then proceeded to dump pills into his mouth.

"Oh, wait, you're only supposed to take one," she said, trying to grab it.

He leaned away from her and began to crunch his mouthful. She managed to get the bottle from him with only slightly swerving the car over the edge of the road. "Spit them out. It's too much!"

"It feels like the right dose to me," he said.

She hesitated. "Have you taken it before?"

"Many times. The crew that brought us here supplied the compound to us on the ship and told us how we could find the same substance on Earth should we have need of more. It is what changes our color to that of humans." He took another bite of the hot dog and then set it on his lap as he pulled out of the jacket. "I will need more of it to remain blended in. These clothes are too warm to wear."

"The robbery," Elle said. "It was baby aspirin."

"In Denver. It is in Colorado. You said you thought my brothers were in Colorado. We now know where to find them."

"Did you tell the scientists about the baby aspirin?" Elle hadn't been there when the scientists did their thing. She wasn't sure what happened. Part of her didn't want to know.

"I did not speak to them. They flashed lights at me and took my fluids."

"Good, that means they—"

A loud siren cut off her words seconds before blue and red lights began to flash. She swore as she looked in the rearview mirror. "We're being pulled over." She looked around the car in a panic. "Put on your seatbelt. Hurry. And don't say anything."

She grabbed her seatbelt and made a show of latching it, so he could see what to do. It took him a moment, but he did it.

"Let me do the talking," she said as she rolled down the window. It stuck a little and she had to pull down on the glass.

"License, registration, proof of insurance." The cop leaned over and peered into the car. He shone a flashlight at Elle then Ice.

"Ah, sure thing," she glanced at the man's nametag, "Officer Beckstead."

Elle reached into her back jeans pocket where she'd stuck her cards. When they were leaving the facility, she hadn't been able to take her purse with her. She handed him her license and smiled. "Is there a problem?"

"Is this your vehicle, ma'am?" The cop was unaffected by her smile.

"No. I borrowed it from a friend," she said.

"Wait here. I'm going to need that registration." He walked toward his cruiser.

"Just stay calm," Elle told Ice.

She reached for the glove box, hoping whoever owned the car had the right paperwork. Otherwise, she wasn't sure how she was getting out of this one.

When she opened the glove box, a gun slipped out and fell on the floor at Ice's feet.

She gasped, glancing back to see if Officer Beckstead had noticed. He hadn't as he was walking back from his car while talking into the walkie-talkie on his shoulder. She couldn't hear what he said.

A packet of white powder remained in the glove box. She didn't need to know what it was to know there was no explaining her way out of driving with a gun and narcotics. Panic filled her. She slammed the glove box shut. "Looks like she doesn't have any registration in the car."

"Please step out, ma'am," the officer said.

She motioned at Ice to stay where he was.

"Is there a problem?" she asked again as she complied. Had he seen the drugs?

"Janet Darcy?"

"No, I'm Elle—"

"This car is registered to Janet Darcy, wanted for drug possession by the state of Utah. I'm going to need you to come with me until we can clear up the matter of why you're in this car." Officer Beckstead placed his hand on his gun and turned his hip away from her as he motioned she should walk to the front of the car.

Her eyes met Ice's through the window. He unfastened his belt. She shook her head in denial.

"Sir, I'll need you to stay put," the officer ordered.

"I think there has been a mistake. My name is—"

"Unfortunately, the computers don't sync up too well out here. We'll need to take you in to verify who you are. Place your hand on the hood of the car, ma'am." Officer Beckstead didn't wait for her to do so before he gave her back a small push. She fell forward. He began tapping her waist with one hand. "Do you have anything on you I need to know about?"

An alien from outer space?

"No, I—"

Her words were cut off as Ice threw open the car door. "Unhand my woman."

"Sir, get back into the car," Officer Beckstead ordered, stretching out his hand and taking a step back. He unlatched his gun holster in warning. She turned to watch him but kept her hands on the car.

Ice lifted the gun that had fallen out of the glove box. "You do not touch my woman in ways she does not like."

"Don't," Elle ordered. "Let me handle this."

But really, it was too late. Ice had a gun on a law enforcement officer. There was no coming back from that. He'd be arrested, put into the system, exposed for what he was.

"You don't want to do this," Officer Beckstead warned.

"Shit," Elle swore under her breath. She pushed off the car, spinning on her heels. She used the momentum to add strength to her punch as she knocked the officer square in the jaw.

Her knuckles cracked. He stumbled in surprise.

"I'm sorry." She hit him a second time. As he fell, she reached forward to catch him. She stumbled under his weight. "Ice, help me get him to his car."

Ice lifted the man and hefted him over his shoulder. He strode toward the police cruiser. Elle ran ahead of him and opened the driver-side door. She found her ID on a small clipboard and grabbed it before turning to the computer. Her name and the car info had been typed in, but it didn't look as if he'd saved the information. She hit the delete key.

"No dashboard cam," she said. She tore the paper copy of her information off his clipboard. "Let's hope he didn't tell the station my name or license number."

Elle wasn't sure how long her luck would hold out. She flexed her sore hand. There were so many ways this could go wrong—*had* gone wrong.

"We need to ditch this car," Elle said, leading the way back to the Ford. "Another officer could be on the way. They'll issue an alert when they figure out what we did, making us Utah's most wanted for assaulting an officer. The Milano Foundation is undoubtedly tracking us, and this little stunt will help them zero in on our location." She opened the door and slid into the seat. She slammed the door shut and turned the screwdriver in the ignition. "Oh, and we probably have drug dealers after us."

"What are drug dealers?" he asked, slamming the door shut as she had.

"Criminals who will be looking for that gun and that bag of coke, or crank, or heroin, or whatever it is. They were probably using this car as some kind of drop point. I doubt they expected someone would want to steal this piece of crap."

She put the car into gear and stepped on the gas, speeding down the dark highway. The policeman's lights blinked in the rearview.

You really fucked things up this time, Elle.

10

Ice held the bag Elle told him to carry as they quickly crossed the parking lot of what she called a truck stop. They'd left the car in a darkened corner of the lot. She'd made him wait outside of the complex as she went in. He did not like being the lookout. The baby aspirin took a while to work, and she said after the police car incident they'd be looking for a blue man accompanying a female.

Giant vehicles towered over them as they passed through the narrow aisles between. Bearded men lifted white sticks to their mouths and blew smoke into the air.

"Hey, sweetheart, you lost?" a man called.

"Not interested," Elle yelled, not bothering to look at who spoke to her.

Ice came out from behind a semi-truck's cab. A man stopped mid-stride on his way to following Elle. He quickly averted his eyes and turned when he saw Ice.

"We're looking for a truck with a red logo that reads 'Pan Darrell' on the side." Elle quickened her pace.

"Are we stealing another car?"

"We're going to stow away in one of the trailers. The Pan Darrell driver told me his next stop is Boulder. That's right outside of Denver. I went around and told everyone I was looking for a ride. I had two offers, but the first one was sketchy and smelled like he hadn't bathed in a while. The second one only had room for one passenger in his cab, and I think he wanted to trade sex for travel. He said he was leaving in twenty minutes, so we don't have much time. We are going to have to sneak onto the back of his truck." She glanced at Ice. "Do you know how to read English?"

Ice nodded. "It was part of my uploads."

"Uploads?" She continued her search.

"The Galaxy Brides aliens inject the information into our brain so that we may have the knowledge. Once it processes, we are able to possess a new skill." Ice noticed a long white truck with a red cab. The rounded logo looked as if it said the words she was looking for. "Is that it?"

"You let someone inject a whole language into your brain, so you could come to Earth and meet women?" She frowned at him. "That seems extreme."

"Actually, they injected two." Ice paused, accessing the ability to add in the gurgling nuances of the Venimice. "*Though we didn't need the first one.*"

"That's the noise you were making when we," she paused before finishing, "found you."

"When you and your friends captured me and took me to a laboratory?" he offered.

Elle stiffened as if he'd insulted her. "They're not my friends. They're people I was hired to work with. If I had known that aliens were real, that *you* were real, I would never have taken the job. I'm sorry."

"I'm not. If you had not taken the job, I would not be free right now. You would not be my girlfriend."

His comment made her laugh, and he smiled. He liked her laughter. It was better than the worry that had been lining her features since the policeman pushed her onto the hood of the stolen car. Even now, he pictured the panicked look on her face as the man patted his hand against her. No one would touch his woman without her permission. Ice would not allow it.

"Why do you all want to marry so badly, anyway?" she asked. "Oh, crap, that's the driver." She pointed at a man in a red jacket coming down one of the aisles. "Hurry."

Elle ran around to the back of the truck and pulled a pin from the bottom of the door. Throwing a lever to the side, she lifted it by small degrees before leaning around the side of the truck. "Get in."

Ice felt cold air hit him, and he sighed in relief. Finally, some reprieve from the heat. He set the bag inside and leaned forward. He then braced his foot to push through the narrow door space on his stomach. Inside, he stood, looking around. Small blue lights illuminated the white walls. Brown boxes wrapped in clear plastic were stacked along the side walls and held into place by yellow ties. The cold felt great against his skin. He didn't realize how badly he'd missed the feel of it. Even his wounds began to tingle.

"He's almost here. Pull me in," Elle said. Her hand darted beneath the door. He didn't hesitate as he grabbed her and slid her along the floor. He then pushed the door shut, trying to be quiet as he forced it down. The sound of the latch falling into place clicked and he let go.

"Wait, don't," Elle cried, hurrying to the door and pulling on it. She couldn't get it to move. "We have to get out of here."

"Why?" Ice turned to look at the cargo. He leaned closer. It was hard to read in the dim light, but he made out a few of the words. "Are chicken patties dangerous?"

Her breath came out in tiny puffs of air and she gripped his arms. "This is a refrigeration truck. They get down to like negative twenty degrees Fahrenheit."

He took a deep breath and smiled. This would be a very pleasant journey.

Elle squeezed him tightly. "Ice, I'll die at negative twenty. Humans can't be that cold. I need a heat source."

She again tried to pull at the door. The trailer began to vibrate and rock. Seeing her panic, he tried to help. The door wouldn't move.

"What are we going to do?" She hurried

toward the front of the truck and began striking it with her hands, yelling, "Hey, we're in here!"

Cold air blasted from a grate next to her.

She fell back, lifting her arms as if they could protect her from the gust of air. Ice pulled the jacket from his shoulders and wrapped it around her own. The truck rocked. Her yelling did not alert anyone.

As good as the cold air felt against his skin, he could tell it had the opposite effect on Elle. She trembled violently. He looked around, finding cloth tarps piled near the wall beneath the air conditioning unit. He pulled them toward the back of the truck and piled them against the boxes, away from the air.

Ice sat on the floor and motioned at her. "Come. I have heat."

"We have...to get...out...of...here," she said through chattering teeth.

"I have heat for you," he repeated.

"Ice, I—"

"Come." This time the word was stern. He motioned to his lap.

Elle inched closer to him, rocking as the truck swayed to the left. She stumbled a little, and he caught her hand.

She gasped, clutching his arm with icy fingers. "You're...warm." She practically fell against him as she knelt on the ground. "You're like...a fire."

When she burrowed into his chest, he reached for her hips and lifted her onto his lap. Her legs straddled him. He would have to deal with the discomfort of their position if it meant helping her. He did not wish for her to die. "No. I believe fire melts ice quickly. I do not."

Elle's head rested against his shoulder. He felt her breath on his neck. His body began to vibrate with need, even as she shivered in his arms. By small degrees, the temperature of her body warmed.

"Thank you," she whispered against his neck.

"I will share my warmth with you anytime, Elle," he answered. "You are my girlfriend."

"I don't think that means what you think it means," Elle said, "but right now, I'd agree to anything so long as you don't let go."

Ice had no intention of releasing her. Ever.

11

ELLE WAS UNSURE HOW LONG SHE'D LAIN against Ice's body, but the warmth had called to her, lulling her to sleep. The smell of Fall filled each breath. She awoke still pressed tightly against him, her legs wedged on either side of his. He was stroking her thighs as if instinctively warming them with his hands. They were on a bumpy road as the truck drove over construction grooves.

Her breasts tingled with awareness and she arched her back to pull her chest away from him. The movement did not have the desired effect as the vibrating against her nipples became more pronounced. It was then she realized it wasn't the truck that vibrated. It was Ice.

She pushed back, not as bothered by the cold air as before. Ice's bright blue eyes stared at her. She glanced down. It was hard to see anything in the shadows. The vibrations came in steady waves, pulsing in an even tempo.

Without thinking her actions through, she kissed him.

The hands on her thighs stilled and tightened. Where his lips had been cool before, they were now warm, as if his body activated in the cold. She moaned softly, parting her lips as she deepened the kiss. He tasted like an exotic spice, slightly familiar, and yet not at the same time. She pulled back, licking her lips.

"Why did you kiss me?" he asked.

"Why did you let me?" She didn't wait for an answer as she kissed him again. Their mouths met in a testing rhythm. Elle knew kissing an alien was, perhaps, strange and wrong and so many other things, but she couldn't stop. Her mouth was drawn to his, just as her body was drawn to his heat.

He pulled on her hips, and she stiffened in a moment of panic. She pressed her hands to his chest. She took several deep breaths, trying to bring rational thought back to her hazed brain.

"Are we...?" She glanced down. The truck continued down the road, swaying as it took a curve.

"I am assured we are compatible humanoids. We would not have been brought here otherwise. I hope that is true because I cannot take much more vibration." Ice pushed up on her hips, urging her to stand. "I will show you."

Elle shivered from being away from his heat. Ice stood and tugged the dark pants down his legs and took the shirt off. An erection stood from his hips. The head was narrower than a human male's, and tiny bumps moved beneath the skin. Curious, she reached to touch the blue member with the tip of a finger.

The bumps were the source of the vibration.

"Do you have a place for it?" Ice's words were pained.

She thought about lying. Could she go through with this?

Her body's reaction said yes, but since when did she let her body make decisions for her brain?

"Is this where you would like me to place it?" Ice touched her opened mouth, slipping a finger in as if to test the entryway.

Elle reached to unbutton her jeans. She

pulled his probing finger from her mouth and placed it down the front of her pants. "My place is here."

Heat enveloped her sensitive clit. Her breathing became ragged as she tried to remain standing. The shock of cold and heat made her lightheaded. He dug his fingers against her soft folds, slipping downward. "I do not feel where I should—" Then his finger slid into her, and he made a small noise. He moved it around, stroking the walls of her sex before nodding. "Yes, that place will do very well. Expose it for me."

Elle wasn't sure what to think of the alien sex talk. It was half-commanding, half-begging. She trembled, looking at his blue skin, debating. She could stop this now. "It's so cold in here."

"I have heat for you."

Heaven help her, she didn't want to stop.

Elle inelegantly took off her shoes and pants. He lowered to his knees before her, instantly pressing his face forward to examine what she had to offer. His breath fanned over her sex, tickling her as it blew the hairs guarding her opening. He petted her with the tip of his finger.

"I have never seen hair here." He brushed his lips over her, and then a hot tongue flicked along the folds. The truck hit a bump, causing his face to press against her more fully. She gasped, grabbing his black hair. She pushed him back so that he fell against the boxes.

Elle went to him, seeking heat, seeking relief from the turmoil building in her wet sex. She straddled his waist, not hesitating like before as she brushed the tip of his vibrating member along her ready body. He grabbed the shaft, aiming it as he braced his other hand and lifted his hips off the floor.

Elle dropped onto Ice's quivering shaft. The clamp of her sex did not stop the vibrations. If anything, they intensified.

"Your cave is so soft," he said, moving his hips in tiny circles. His eyes closed, and he moaned. "I enjoy being inside." Elle lifted to stroke herself against him and his eyes instantly opened. "Please, don't release me. I am not done vibrating."

Elle's gaze met his pleading one, and she dropped back down. Oh, fuck, but it felt good. He sighed in relief and restarted the tiny circular movements. Her hands gripped his shoulders. The blue flesh fascinated her and she couldn't look away.

"This is how we Earthlings do it." Elle lifted up and bore down, stroking his length.

"That is...strange." He seemed to consider the motion.

"It's how you make *me* vibrate," she tried to explain as she felt her climax approaching.

Elle couldn't believe it. She was having sex with an alien. And it was freaking awesome.

Ice slowly mimicked her rhythm. By small degrees, a smile crossed his features. "And this is how you like—"

"Oh, yes," she interrupted, riding him harder. "This is how I like it."

Tremors erupted inside her belly, causing her to stiffen on him as she met with release. The intense pleasure filled her. She cried out softly and was unable to move.

Ice gripped her hips, holding her against him. The vibration of his shaft pulsed harder, sending what felt like tiny shocks of electricity into her. His climax caused a jolt of energy to flow out from him into her. Strange alien words left his lips. The energy made her skin tingle with awareness, but it also warmed her, giving her an inner heat that had not been there before.

They both tried to catch their breath. She no longer noticed the cold.

"I will enjoy vibrating you again," he whispered, kissing the curve of her neck. "Many times."

Elle knew that she was going to let him do just that.

WHATEVER HAPPENED when they met their sexual climaxes had infused her with enough heat to feel comfortable in the impossibly cold temperatures. But the feeling did not last, and after an hour she felt the cold trying to creep in. Ice held her in his arms, not bothering to cover himself. His shaft stayed partially erect as if that were its natural state.

Elle ran her chilled fingers along his inner thigh. "I think I need you to vibrate me again. I'm starting to freeze."

Instantly, his body responded, gently at first but when she touched his member, the bumps engorged along the shaft to press against her hand. The vibrations intensified.

"You showed me the Earth way. I will show

you the Sintazian way now." He stood up. Her hand fell away from him. He motioned that she should join him.

Elle stood, and he turned her away from him. Then, pushing at her back, he lowered the top half of her body forward. She grabbed the boxes to keep from falling. The truck continued to sway and bump. He took her hips in his hands and shoved himself into her sex. He stayed deep, working his hips in tight, fast circles. The hardened bumps hit her just right, and she cried out as she gripped the boxes tighter. The cold stung her fingers, but she didn't care.

He spoke his alien language, the sound like a song she couldn't understand. As he remained seated inside her, he leaned into her ass. The vibrations worked their way up his stomach to spread over her from the back as well.

As much as she wanted him to slam himself into her with hard thrusts, she had to admit there was something to be said for the steady vibrating motion.

"Now I will do your Earth way." Ice pulled out and thrust. Elle made a weak noise of surprise. He did it again. "This Earth way is enjoyable."

"Ah, fuck," was the only response she could manage.

All she could do was hold on as he took her from behind. He had her under his complete control. The zaps of electricity started. She climaxed hard. He kept riding her, drawing out the tremors racking her body. Then, the final burst of energy shot through her. Heat infused her, and she pushed weakly to standing. He slipped out of her body.

Elle lifted her arms around his neck and leaned her face close to his. "Had I known you'd make me feel like this, I'd have helped you escaped weeks ago."

"Had I known I'd find you, I would not have protested coming to Earth," he answered.

Elle moved her mouth closer to his so that their lips brushed as they spoke. "Had I known I'd be expending this much energy, I would have had us stow away on a snack cake truck."

12

Ice hoped the truck would never stop. If infusing his woman to keep her alive held so much pleasure, he never wanted it to end. Galaxy Brides had been vague on the human mating customs, only to say that Sintazian and Earthlings were physically compatible. He never imagined there would be so much writhing and thrusting involved.

Seriously, why hadn't his people thought of this technique? Usually, they pressed together and vibrated, but she didn't vibrate unless he made her, and even then, it was more trembling and jerking. Ice liked the challenge it presented. He wanted to do it again.

"This trip has to be over soon," Elle said, her

teeth beginning to chatter a little, "and he'll check the load, so we can get out of here."

Ice felt mildly guilty as he sat naked, enjoying the temperatures. His wounds had healed, and he felt better than he had since leaving his home planet.

"I'm sorry," she said, pressing her cold ear against his arm for heat. "This is the worst rescue attempt ever. I should have come up with a better plan."

"You freed me. That is all that matters. This plan has not been bad." Ice tried to comfort her, though he wasn't entirely truthful. He found very little about his trip to Earth to be good. He'd found *her*, that was the one sunny spot in an otherwise shadowy experience, but he had lost his brothers, and he might never see them or go home again.

He longed for the isolation and silence of the ice plains. Earth had so many noises—voices, buzzing lights, beeps and dings, jingling bells over doors, grumbling engines. This planet was a chaos of sound and movement.

Chaos had not been a good surname choice. He should have been called Ice Silence. That is what he wanted. Yes, Sintaz was lonely. His people were leaving the harsh planet for better opportunities, but it was still home. It was safe. It was familiar. Snow and Frost had been there where he could protect them. He longed to go back.

But what about Elle? Her frail human body would not survive the Sintazian winter without meticulous preparations. As much as he liked infusing her with heat that wasn't exactly practical on a daily basis. He'd have to hunt for their food, tend to other chores. She'd spend half the year in an ESC snowsuit. He couldn't stop every earth hour to warm up a wife.

His body stirred, giving a completely different opinion on the matter. "Shall I warm you again?"

"I'm so tired," she mumbled, shivering. "I just want to sleep."

It appeared that their mating had been a temporary fix. He held her closer, willing her to take his body heat. She looked as if she wanted to open her eyes but couldn't. Her lashes fluttered.

Her hand dropped weakly from his chest onto his lap. She slumped against him. This didn't feel right.

"Elle?"

She didn't answer.

Ice had never put clothes on a woman, but it wasn't exactly glacier excavation. He grabbed her clothing and began slipping them over her body. Then, he took his clothes and added that over the top, tying the pants beneath her chin around her head to cover her ears. He held her tight against his body, setting her on his lap so she touched as little of the floor as possible.

"I never meant to hurt anyone," she mumbled.

He didn't understand why she would say such a thing, now, in this place.

Where moments before he'd fantasized about staying in the cold cocoon of the semi-trailer, he now willed it to stop. He had no idea how far it was to Colorado. He kept his eyes open, watching and listening for signs that he should do something more for Elle. He held her hands, then rubbed her legs—anything to give her heat. He even tried kissing her, but she didn't respond.

Ice didn't know what to do—and that terrified him.

If she died, it would be because she'd tried to save him. The burden of that knowledge would rest upon his head.

A small moan left her as if she began to revive herself, but she didn't speak or look at him.

Suddenly, the vehicle shifted, and his tarp seat slid over the metal floor. He caught his feet on the door, still holding her. The engine cut out even though the sound of the refrigeration unit still hummed.

He heard faint noises, much different from the sounds of travel. Ice kicked the back door, reverberating it. He kicked it again, and again. Someone fumbled with the latch, and he stood, not caring that he was naked as he held Elle in his arms.

The door slowly lifted and a scared voice yelled, "Who's in there?"

Ice kicked the door upward, forcing it to lift all the way. The man in the red jacket stared at him in surprise. His mouth worked, but no sound came out.

"We are going to a costume party in the desert," Ice stated. He leapt out of the cargo hold, still holding Elle. City lights surrounded them like tiny dots over the night landscape. The truck had stopped in a nearly abandoned parking lot near similar vehicles.

Ice strode toward a metal fence. The warm air counteracted the warmth of his body and he felt himself cooling. When he looked back, it was to see the driver pulling a small container out of his pocket. He glanced at Ice, and then the bottle, before throwing the item far away from him.

Ice walked along the fence until he found an opening. No one was around to witness their escape from the truck besides the driver, so he kept walking, unsure as to where he would end up, but knowing it was best he kept moving.

ELLE FELT LIKE SHE'D BEEN RUN OVER BY A tank and dumped in the bottom of a bog. Everything hurt, some parts from the hard ground she now lay on and some from the sex marathon in a refrigerated semi-trailer.

She laughed before even opening her eyes. None of this seemed real, and she thought for a moment she'd be waking from a dream.

Instead of a warm bed, she found herself staring at the inside of a box. Her feet stuck out the open end. The dirty smell of city streets wafted over her.

She felt movement beside her. Ice had rolled up her sleeve and was studying the inside of her elbow.

What in the world...?

He adjusted his weight and held up a small syringe. It took a moment for her to realize he meant to inject her with whatever it was.

Elle flailed, coming to life as she slammed the hand holding the needle and jerked away from him. "Stop! What are you doing?"

He looked at her, his eyes so blue they almost took on a surreal glow in the dim light. "The man said it would make you feel all right."

"What man?" She tried to push up but was weak. "Where are we? What happened to the truck? How long have we been here?"

She eyed her arms, making sure there were no marks from having been shot up.

"The man who took the paper from your pocket and said that this place with the other circus freaks would be safe because the cops never bother junkie row as long as we don't front and keep cool. I told him I was, in fact, cool, so he traded with me for the magic cure to fix what ailed you."

Realizing what had probably happened, she felt her pockets. The wad of cash was gone.

"He said it was the best this side of the border," Ice assured her. Before admitting, "I do not know which border. It was supposed to wake you up and give you energy."

Elle frowned as she crawled her way out of the box into a dim alleyway. The light made it look like dawn and a line of people were outside a door with a large sign stating, *FOOD HERE.* Bottles and old syringes littered the alley.

"You gave three hundred dollars to a drug dealer for a cardboard box and a syringe full of poison?" she asked in disbelief. She had her bank card, but by now the Milano team would be tracking it.

"Not poison. Magic," he stated.

"Ice, I want you to listen to me *very* carefully." She reached up to touch his face. "Magic is not real. At least not here on Earth. That was a bad man you talked to. He lies to people. You need to stay away from men like that."

"Blue tattoo man. I see you, blue tattoo." Laughter followed the words.

Elle couldn't tell if the man who approached them was high or drunk, but by the way he swayed, he wasn't operating at full capacity. "Someone wants to talk to you."

"Who?" Elle asked suspiciously. She glanced around. Had someone tracked them down?

Milano or the police? She wasn't sure which was worse. Since they had ditched the car, she doubted the people who owned it could figure out who they were or where they went.

The man pointed at the sky and laughed.

"Get out of here," Elle ordered, waving him away.

Ice was looking up at the sky. "I do not see anyone."

"We need to leave." Elle felt dizzy and sore, but she ignored the pain in her body. Now was not the time for weakness.

Ice held up two syringes. "What should I do with these?"

Elle took them from him and squirted the liquid on the ground. She tossed the needles in a dumpster.

"Blue tattoo man, I see you," the man yelled.

"I see you, too," Ice stated, his loud tone matter-of-fact.

"Stop talking to the crazy man." Elle grabbed Ice's arm and pulled.

She led him out of the alleyway, trying to get her bearings.

"Maybe I do not need to take the baby aspirin. Humans have not been as averse to my coloring as we were led to believe on the ship." Ice held up his arm. The blue color had changed some, darkening, but it still was obviously a non-human tone.

"The police will be looking for a blue man. I think it's best you do whatever it takes to hide." Elle touched his face. His skin was cool, unlike in the refrigeration trailer. "But don't take that to mean I don't like the way you look. I do. If it were up to me, I wouldn't change a thing about you."

"Thank you for those words." He placed his hand over hers, keeping her pressed against his cheek. His jaw was smooth with no stubble. At first, it had been hard to see past the blue, but she saw it less and less as she looked at him, not because of the baby aspirin, but because she felt like she was beginning to see him as something more than an alien from outer space who she needed to save. He didn't grow a beard though he had eyebrows. His black hair had a blue tint to it that only showed when the light hit it. His lips were darker than the rest of his face. He had a strong European nose and distinct eyes that were hard to forget.

"Did your people come from Earth? I'm trying to understand how we look so similar." Elle dropped her hand and led the way in the direction that seemed to have the most activity passing across the sidewalk.

"Many humanoid aliens look as we do. I have heard speculation as to why that is, but I don't think anyone really has the answer. Sometimes—I believe you call it genetics—sometimes those match up and sometimes they do not."

He walked alongside her, and for a moment she felt as if everything was normal. He was a man. She was a woman. This was simply a stroll.

But that feeling didn't last, as she thought of all the things threatening them—the Milano Foundation, the police, not to mention various government agencies that would kill to get an alien in custody.

"If that's true, why come here? Earth can't be the most welcoming planet you could find. There have to be better places out there to look for wives." Elle didn't want to admit how much she was already falling for him. Feelings rarely paid attention to logic. But there was no way this would work. She couldn't leave Earth. She wasn't brave enough to take that kind of journey. And Ice shouldn't stay. It wasn't safe for him. "What is Sintaz like?"

She'd like to picture him there, at home with

his family, happy. One thing was for sure, she would never look at the stars the same way again.

He smiled, and she thought she saw longing in his expression.

"You miss it, don't you?" Hunger gnawed at her stomach, and she desperately wanted to eat and sleep. She was tempted to find a hotel, any hotel so that she could crash face first on a mattress.

"I miss the quiet. Earth is full of noise." He glanced around the abandoned sidewalk as they continued past old brick buildings. "Like now."

"I don't hear anything." She tried to detect the same sound he did.

"The lights hum." He pointed to an industrial light that had been left on. If she concentrated, she could hear a little bit of an electrical hum. "It is a constant. Earth is full of engines, and beeps, and clicks as people walk. My home world is quiet, more so now that my people have left the planet for other star systems." He stopped walking. "I wish to bring you there, but I do not think you will survive."

"The flight there?" Elle furrowed her brow in confusion. "Is it dangerous?"

"I'm talking about the weather. Sintazian

nights are colder than the refrigerator truck. After seeing your reaction, I don't think you would survive the temperatures." This conclusion appeared to sadden him. "I worry that I would not be able to warm you as often as you would need."

The nerves in her stomach did a little jump of anticipation as she recalled how he had kept her from freezing to death. Even now she wanted him. She pushed down the desire. Ice needed her to think. He clearly wasn't ready for Earth life. He trusted all the wrong people.

Elle didn't want to leave for another planet. She'd miss her parents and her brother. She might not see them too often, but it was nice knowing they were there. Still, his certainty that they couldn't be together stung. She wasn't ready to end whatever was happening between them.

She resigned herself to the truth. There was no use protesting. He was an alien. She was a human. This relationship had been doomed even before it started.

"I don't understand why you came here for brides if you're not able to stay with them." Elle wasn't sure why she asked. It wasn't like she wanted to get married. That would be beyond insane, right?

Right?

"My brothers were excited to meet women, and Galaxy Alien Mail Order Brides corporation made promises they should not have." Ice's steps slowed, and she noticed his shoulders slump forward.

"Just your brothers?"

"I didn't dare hope that I would find someone on such a journey. I thought they promised more than they could deliver, but I did not think they would abandon us here." His breathing deepened. "How did you know where to find us? Did Galaxy Brides set us up?"

"I was told where to be." Elle didn't have a better answer for him.

A dot of rain hit his lips, and they both looked up. Another drop hit under her eye. The cold moisture stung and when she brought her face down, it rolled over her cheek like a tear. Flashing lights and the rumble of thunder warned them of a coming storm.

"My guess is Foundation scientists found a way to track the ship—" A loud crack cut off her words. The sound jolted her a little.

Ice became rigid.

"Under there." Elle motioned that they should

duck into shelter to get out of the rain, but when she tried to lift her foot, it wouldn't move. Pain shot along her body, and she inhaled sharply. Moisture gathered on her side, sticking her shirt to her skin. Stunned, she reached for it. Her fingers slipped in blood. She touched it again, pushing her fingers into the wound. "I...I think someone shot me."

Elle fell toward Ice, unable to control her body.

He lifted her into his arms. "What do I do?"

"Run."

"I SEE YOU, BLUE TATTOO!" The strange man with the smelly breath popped out of an inlet as Ice ran with Elle down the sidewalk toward the box house encampment. "I see you!"

Two armed fighters in black clothing appeared next to the man, shoving the shouting man out of their way. The larger one he knew from the facility. Luther liked to taunt and kick him when he'd been tied up. The men charged toward Ice, carrying handguns.

"Don't move," they warned. "Put her down and come with us."

"Run," Elle mumbled again.

Ice pulled her closer. Her arm flopped down, away from her body.

The armed fighter he did not recognize came at him a little too fast. That confidence would be the man's downfall.

Ice pivoted and kicked out his leg while still holding Elle. She moaned in protest, but her body gave no resistance to the movement. Ice's foot met with the man's stomach, doubling him over even as it sent him stumbling back into his partner. A weapon dropped on the ground, skittering over the concrete.

The smelly man dove from where they attackers pushed him and grabbed the weapon.

"Run, blue tattoo, run," the man yelled as he fired the gun into the sky. Shots rang off several times.

Ice ran. Elle bled onto his arm. The metallic smell was new to him, but unmistakable. She stopped moaning, and he feared he would lose her. There was no help he could give. If she were Sintazian, he'd put her in the cold and slow down the process as she had time to heal, but she was human, and in many ways they were much more fragile.

His mind raced as he tried to think of an Earth word for helping wounds. He knew there were places, not unlike the medical booths those reticulan missionaries offered some planets. The Sintaz population had no use for them, but had they been offered to Earth? Nothing in his language knowledge led him to believe it was an option.

"Veterinary physician," he said suddenly as the word came to him. That was a person who helped injuries and diseases. Physicians were doctors. That is what he needed. A veterinarian. "Don't worry, Elle, I won't let you die."

14

ELLE GROANED. THE MEDICINE-INDUCED HAZE that had followed her since surgery numbed her senses, but not the pain. It was beginning to creep back into her side. A blur of a blue figure moved past the open doorway. The image made her try to call out to Ice. Her voice croaked, and the sound was not coherent.

Elle became aware of something on her face, and she slapped her fingers against the nasal cannula inserted into her nose. She roughly pulled it off and slung the oxygen tubing over the bedrail. Her vision wasn't steady as she looked first at the IV fluid being fed into her arm, and then at the blipping heart monitor mounted on the wall above her head.

Another blue figure moved past the door. She tried to push up, even as she realized it was a nurse and not Ice. Before even looking, she knew he wasn't in the room. What had happened? How did she get here?

Seeing her struggling to sit up, one of the nurses turned into the room. He smiled at her. "Good to see you're awake."

"Ice," she said, a little dazed from the medicine. Annoyed, she pawed at the tape securing the IV on her arm.

"Elle, please don't to that," the nurse said. "If you pull out your IV, I'll have to re-stick you in order to give you your pain medication."

She squinted to look at his name tag, partially obscured by the stethoscope dangling from his neck. "Bob."

He followed her gaze down and then said, "Rob."

"Ice," she insisted. Was he there? Was he shot? Did he get away? She had to know.

Rob gently pushed her back down, not giving her a choice, and reinserted the oxygen cannula back into place. "I need to check a few things then I'll get you some ice chips." He lifted the side of her gown to look at her dressing then turned his attention to the monitor. He nodded. "Looking good. No more bleeding. Your vital signs are stable."

"Where...?" She tried to ask where Ice was.

"You're in the Intensive Care Unit at—"

"I have to go." Elle tried to pull the cannula off again.

"Elle, try to relax. You've just gotten out of surgery and you're in no condition to go anywhere. Do you have someone I can call for you? A friend? A husband?" Rob again adjusted the nasal cannula.

Elle blinked several times, trying to clear her thoughts. She eyed the nurse as she tried to get out of bed. He had kind eyes that stared out from a rounded face. His short hair looked to have migrated from his balding head to his chin. She fought but Rob's firm hold sapped her energy and she finally stopped trying to sit up.

"Ice," she whispered.

He let her go and patted her arm. "There you go. Just relax. You're safe now. The police are right outside ICU and no one can hurt you here. They need to ask you a few questions about the shooting. Do you think you're up to talking to them yet?"

That kept her from falling back into a drugged haze. Police? Did they come to arrest her for assault? Did they have Ice?

She lifted her hands, reassuring herself she wasn't cuffed to the bed.

"There's nothing to worry about," Rob said. "It's all routine. The sooner they get your information, the sooner they can find who did this to you."

"I can't…" Elle wanted him to understand. She couldn't be here.

"I know you've gone through a lot today but it's important that you work with us. Besides getting shot, you arrived with cold-exposure injuries to your toes and fingers. Your toes especially showed signs of first-degree frostbite."

Elle tried to look at her toes but the blanket hid them. "I can't…"

"You might not feel them, but I promise, they're still there. You're a very lucky lady. Any longer and you could have lost them. We treated the blisters and you should regain feeling in them when the painkillers wear off, but we don't want them to wear off too quickly, do we?" He pulled a pre-filled morphine syringe—and alcohol swab packet from his pocket.

"Don't," she protested. "I can't be here. I have to go."

"Right now, the only thing you have to do is rest. Your body has been through a lot. It needs time to heal." He uncapped the syringe. "Do you think you're up to talking to the police and telling them what happened?"

She shook her head and mumbled gibberish, closing her eyes.

"I'll tell them they have to wait until this morphine wears off a little bit." He injected medicine into her IV and she instantly felt heavy.

I need Ice.

15

Ice kept his head down as someone walked past him. The jacket was wet from the rain, but he didn't care. His thoughts were elsewhere.

Elle. She'd been so weak, so pale, so covered in red. If he were to unzip the jacket, he'd see her blood staining his clothes.

Ice hoped she would be all right. He needed her to be all right. If she died that would be on him. Though, he might never know her fate.

Elle would not like him talking to strange men, but he had no choice. He needed guidance around the city, and news of the aspirin thieves had spread through the Denver street people. One had even made reference to a blue man being involved. Ice glanced at his off-colored hands. His skin had finally changed from blue to more of a brown-tan.

"Yeah, man, my cousin was there. Said he saw one of them. Said he was painted from head to toe with blue paint," the man had said before billowing an interesting-smelling smoke from his lips. His brown pants were stained at the knees and his t-shirt had holes in it. "Very hippy, man. I bet they were like saving babies or something with it."

The woman with the smoker had insisted the aspirin thief was just a stupid criminal, and that the cousin was a liar because there was no way the robber was blue. The news would have reported that. The two bickered a little over the details, but in the end, the woman had been a little more helpful in pointing him in the direction he needed to go to find the pharmacy in question.

He looked up at the sign, Junior's Pharmacy, and knew he was in the right place. The building was where the woman described it—next to a blue dumpster with a bright orange happy face painted on the side.

Ice tried to look at the building from all angles before going toward the door. He detected none of the fighters who'd attacked them. He walked in and looked around. The small store had rows of bottles and boxes. The cracked floor tiles were clean but discolored in spots. Seeing a man in a white coat behind a glass shield, he approached him. The man was much shorter than Ice, and he could see the top of his gray head more than his downturned face. The word "pharmacist" was scrolled across the chest.

"Can I help you?" The pharmacist did not look up.

Ice placed his hand on the counter a little too hard to get the man's full attention. "I am looking for the men who took your aspirin."

At that, the pharmacist looked up at him. "Excuse me?"

"I need to find the men who took your baby aspirin." Ice didn't move his hand.

"Are you some kind of private investigator?" The pharmacist shook his head, turned back to what he'd been doing and finished jotting down a notation before moving toward a shelf.

Belatedly, Ice lied. "Yes."

"I can't help you. They took some cases of aspirin, that's all. I reported it to the police because insurance doesn't pay out unless there's a report, but other than that, there isn't much call to find a couple of whack-a-doodles when generic baby aspirin isn't exactly the narcotic authorities care about."

"I must find them. They are my brothers," Ice said.

"So you're not a private investigator?" The pharmacist put down a container and came back to the window.

"No. I am a man looking for his brothers. They need help." Ice had no idea if honesty was the best route, but he didn't have any experience lying to humans to get information.

"You do resemble them." The man nodded. "Listen, I get it. My son has the same struggles with addiction. He's a good kid, but those demons are hard to fight." He leaned closer to the speaking holes in the glass and said, "Your brothers didn't hurt anyone. It's like I told that news reporter. They were the politest criminals I'd ever seen. One even apologized and said he needed it. I don't know what they were planning on doing with that much baby aspirin, or if they were confused, but my insurance covered the theft." He reached beneath the counter and held up an envelope. "Three days later, I found this shoved under my back door. It's filled with cash. I have no idea what the writing on it means, but I can only guess it's payment for the cases and the candy bars. Honestly, if that is the case, this is more than they were worth. I can't think of anyone else who would want to give me money. I haven't been sure what to do with it because I don't know where it came from."

Ice leaned closer to the glass. "May I see the writing?"

The pharmacist glanced at his hand and moved his fingers aside. "It's just some symbol."

It was them. A tight knot released the hold it had on his stomach and he breathed easier than he had in a long time. He'd found them. The writing was as familiar to him as his own hand. It was the Sintazian words for "*please forgive.*"

"It says they are sorry," Ice said. "My brothers are not thieves. They would not have wanted you to suffer a loss at their hands."

The pharmacist took a deep breath, glanced around, and then slid the envelope under a small rectangular opening cut in the glass. "I can see you're worried. Insurance paid for the loss. I'm not sure where they got this much cash, but I can imagine whoever they took it from would be looking for it. I've never taken a strange envelope of cash in return for medicine and, after seeing what my son went through, I don't plan on starting now. I'm going to pretend that I never saw it."

Ice nodded. "Thank you." He looked around, wishing for a sign as to where to go next. He felt so close, and yet so far from finding Snow and Frost.

"I don't know if this is anything, but there are some abandoned buildings about three blocks north." He pointed toward the far end of the store. "You can't miss them. They're the tall red-brick ones. I know several squatters live up in that area. If they're staying around here, that'd be where I looked first."

"Thank you." Ice placed his hand on the glass and nodded before hurrying out of the store.

"Good luck," the man called, the words almost lost as the door shut behind him.

Ice ran toward the abandoned buildings. He didn't pause as he crossed the streets and alleyways. A couple of times, cars screeched to a halt as he cut in front of them, but he didn't care. Every passing second felt like an eternity. The fear he'd felt since watching his brothers run off into the trees culminated in this moment. If he didn't find them now, he might never get the chance.

Or, worse, if he could track them, then the humans who'd imprisoned him might be able to as well. They had already shown up in Denver.

A flash of the last moment he'd seen Elle filtered through his mind. Her eyes had been open, but she didn't see. Her limbs had remained lifeless as she lay on the small metal table. The stunned veterinary physician's mouth had opened, and he stuttered something Ice didn't understand.

"Please fix her," Ice whispered to himself, as he had to that man. "Please fix her. Please fix her."

The buildings were right where the pharmacist had said they'd be. Fires glowed from trashcans as he passed several gatherings of people. Laughter rang out as did shouts of anger and warning. Ice hugged his clothing tighter to him, trying not to be noticed. No one stopped him or even seemed to care who he was or what he was doing.

He studied each face he passed, eyed the builds of the men hidden in the shadows. Desperation filled him each time a group proved to be only humans. He walked faster, intent on moving through each and every building if he had to. If his brothers were here, he'd find them.

"I said I'd pay," a man yelled. The loud crash that followed sent several members of the gathering scurrying away from the noise.

Figures fought in the distance, and Ice angled his fast walk away from them. Well, actually, only one figure seemed to be fighting. The other one flailed in the air as he was held over the man's head.

Just as he was about to rush past, he watched the larger man bend at the knees before throwing his opponent onto an old mattress on the concrete. The man bounced, groaning on impact.

Ice stopped. He ignored the man on the ground as he stared at the winner of the battle.

"Snow?" Ice said, the word not forceful. He knew that fighting stance. He'd *taught* his brothers that fighting stance.

At the sound, his brother turned. The man on the mattress took the opportunity to run. Snow let him go. "Ice?"

The word propelled him into action. He rushed to his brother, lifting his hands to press his fingers to Snow's. They gripped each other's hands tight, leaning their foreheads together in a long greeting.

Words, neither Earthling, nor Venimice, nor Sintazian, couldn't explain the relief he felt in finding his brother alive on a strange, dangerous planet.

Snow pulled away first. "How did you escape? Did they let you go? Did the Galaxy Alien Mail Order Brides crewmen find you?"

Ice answered the question with his own questions. "Is Frost with you? Is he safe? Have you heard from those alien bastards who left us here? Does that man you were fighting have something to do with our being here?"

"That man is a job. I must get money from him to give to the person he owes. It is an easy way to survive. I am not sure why more humans do not do it." Snow took Ice by the arm and led him toward a building. "Frost is here. He does not come out of our home because his body has not been processing the aspirin skin changer. It made him sick and turned him green. We found it easier to hide him from view as we waited for word of your whereabouts."

"Word from who? I was held prisoner in Utah. Scientist wanted to examine me and test me. I have seen them in this city. They are looking for you. We cannot stay here. Humans cannot be trusted." Ice thought of Elle. "*Most* humans cannot be trusted."

"Galaxy Brides has been looking for you since your capture. They contacted us with that device they stuck in that travel pack they gave Snow to carry, but we refused to get on their ship without you. We would not risk them flying us away from here. Frost convinced them that we had connections and if they didn't undo their mistake, we'd have the entire Federation Alliance coming after them."

"And they believed him?" Ice asked in surprise. Sintazians had nothing to do with the Federation.

"He was very convincing." Snow led the way into one of the abandoned buildings and down a narrow set of concrete stairs. The passageway was dark, and Ice kept his eyes on his brother's back. "Help me with this."

Snow leaned over and pushed at a large rock. Ice helped him slide it away from a small door. Once it was clear, Snow opened the door and went inside. Large pipes ran along the ceiling and walls of the stone room. Old material hung from various pipes, somewhat creating a room. Blankets lined the floor, mussed up from having been laid on. It was not their Sintazian home, but the enclosure felt safe.

"Frost! I found him. Ice is here," Snow called.

The sound of movement came from behind a blanket. Frost appeared, his eyes searching until they landed on Ice. He didn't speak as he rushed forward to take his brother's hands. They pressed their heads together and Ice took a deep breath.

"I have found you," Ice whispered.

"I am sorry I insisted we come to this place. The women are not what they promised us, and Earth is not friendly to aliens. I feared my decision had lost you to us forever." Frost leaned his head back. "Did those men harm you?"

Ice wanted to tell them of Elle, and how she'd saved him, but a scraping noise interrupted them.

"Tell us when we are on the ship," Snow said. He went toward the material curtain and tugged it off the pipe.

His brothers had an alien tied to a chair. The stocky creature wore a skin suit over his alien form, but his large head would make it impossible to blend with the humans effectively. His black hair was the same length all around as it hung over his forehead and the tops of his silicone human ears. His hands were pulled out to his sides, tied with rope to pipes to keep them apart. The skin suit hung from his wrists in tatters, showing yellow alien flesh. It was possible the alien had tried to escape and shed part of his disguise in the process.

But it was the silver uniform with the Galaxy Alien Mail Order Brides' logo that gave away who he was.

"This is how you convinced them to help us," Ice concluded with a nod of approval.

"It seemed only fair. One of their brothers in exchange for mine," Frost answered. "The Federation watches bridal procurement very closely and a missing worker would be noted."

"It's time, Gary," Snow stated. "Call the ship and take us home."

16

Elle heard movement before she managed to open her eyes. Someone walked around her hospital room. She tried to lift her hand, but a restraint limited her mobility. The sound of a metal cuff clanked.

She was under arrest.

Elle inhaled sharply, fighting to clear her head.

"Give us a moment with her," someone said.

She knew that voice. Dr. Hanklen.

Her blurry eyes took in the situation. Larson stood in a police uniform. The material stretched on his larger frame. Next to him, Dr. Hanklen wore a suit.

"Fine, but she's still recovering. Don't do

anything to rile her up. She's still my patient until I discharge her, Detective." The doctor spoke to Hanklen.

Detective?

"Don't leave," Elle tried to say, but Larson coughed to cover her voice and Hanklen ushered the doctor out and shut the door.

Elle pushed up on the bed and tugged at her handcuffed wrist. There was no freeing herself. She looked for the call button for help, but Larson swooped forward and pulled the wire. The clip on the button holding it to the blanket snapped as it was jerked out of her reach. He threw it aside.

"Where is he, Elle?" Hanklen demanded.

Elle pressed her hand against the bandage on her side to give the wound support and refused to speak as she inched up on the bed. She knew Ice would go looking for his brothers, but she would never tell them that.

"I know the ship is coming back for them," Hanklen said. "There is no use denying it. Where are they meeting it?"

"I don't know what you're talking about." She turned her eyes accusingly to Larson. "Someone shot me. I've been in the hospital."

"Casualty of war," Larson stated, not

remorseful in the least. If he wasn't the one who'd shot her, he wasn't about to censure the person who did.

"This isn't a war," Elle stated, just to be defiant. She wanted to buy some time so the doctor would come back. She tried to scream, but Hanklen was close enough to grab her mouth to shut her up.

Elle hoped they'd reveal what they had discovered about Ice's whereabouts. If it was true that a ship was coming back for him, then she wanted to make sure he got on it.

"Of course it's a war," Larson countered. "Aliens can't just land on our planet without our permission."

Elle chose to ignore him as she turned her attention to Hanklen. Larson might be two hundred pounds of pure muscle, but Hanklen was the real danger in the room. The scientist was cunning and smart and had shown a blatant disregard for anyone who was not in line with his personal goals.

Hanklen grabbed her chart from the end of the bed and began flipping through it. He stopped on a page, frowning. "Your bloodwork seems a little..." He studied her for a long moment. "What happened? Mind control? Skin toxins? Why did you help him escape? Nothing in your psychological profile indicated you weren't a team player."

Love. Compassion.

Elle didn't answer.

"Larson, call Dr. Petals. I think her patient needs x-rays." Hanklen's gaze stayed on hers. Larson lifted his phone to obey. Elle knew she wasn't going for any kind of scans.

Elle thought to see someone pass by the door and let loose a loud scream for help.

Larson dropped his phone down and lunged for her. He bumped her wound, causing her to cry out as his hand clasped over her mouth. She weakly fought him.

Hanklen pulled a syringe from his jacket and twisted the cap off the needle with his teeth. She reached for the IV tubing, trying to grab it before the doctor had a chance to inject her. But Larson was too strong, and no amount of willpower could counteract the morphine flooding her system.

17

"IF WE ARE WELCOME TO COME TO EARTH TO look for brides, someone forgot to tell the Earthlings about it," Frost said as he led Gary, the captive Galaxy Brides' crewman he'd kidnapped for leverage. Ice doubted Gary was the alien's real name, but then, Ice wasn't really his.

The mountainous countryside echoed with the sound of night animals. Gary insisted the ship would come for them if he ordered it to. Frost had a handheld device in his hand, so the stout alien could do just that once they reached the pickup location.

"If you recall from the contract you signed, there are some risks involved when visiting a new planet. The information packet sent out was very clear that the general Earthling population does not know aliens are real," Gary defended. The hands of his human costume still hung from his wrists. Ice thought about pulling the skin suit off him. As a human, Gary could only be described as creepy. "Didn't you listen to the entire recording?"

"Which part?" Snow asked. "The part where it said to join you for jolly-making on Earth, where the humanoid females were digestible food?"

"Or the part where you said the women were compactible and ready for travel?" Frost added, sliding his hand over the alien's head to force the skin suit to wrinkle on his face. It ripped a little in the back.

Gary reached for his face and pulled at the skin suit around his eyes, ripping it open a little so he could see. "You are not allowed to eat the humans."

"That's not what your recording translator said in Sintazian," Ice answered.

"No. That's all wrong. I was assured those were the best translators on the market." Gary seemed very upset. "We can't have our clients eating humans. This must be addressed at once."

Ice knew that Sintazian translators were often wrong, even the best ones, but he didn't bother to put Gary at ease. The man and his crew had left them behind. It was their fault he'd been captured and brought to the facility where...

Where Elle saved me.

With each step through the shaded mountain path, he felt tension rolling over him. This is what had to happen. He needed to get his brothers home. They had to leave Earth. It wasn't safe.

Yet, he didn't want to go. The thought of Sintaz should have brought him pleasure, but instead he just ached for what could never be.

"Elle would never survive on Sintaz. Why would you even bring us to a place whose inhabitants could not come back with us?" Ice demanded.

"Elle?" Frost asked.

"Arrangements could have been made," Gary said. "There are special domes the humans use when living in Antarctica."

"The place with the fat cookie monster who forces pointy-eared children to work in his factories?" Frost inquired.

"Yes," Gary said. "We would have employed

the same technique on your planet. As long as they only went outside in the advanced ESC frozen-technology snowsuits, they would have been fine."

"Who is Elle?" Snow grabbed Ice's arm, stopping him. "Did you find a woman?"

Ice nodded. "She is the one who freed me from my prison." He looked at Gary. "I need you to locate her, so I know she is well. She was shot trying to help me. The people she took me from were not pleased."

Gary put out his hand for the handheld.

"Is this the location?" Frost asked before giving it over.

Gary nodded. He took the device and said, "I need transport for four and a location transport for a bride named Elle..." Gary looked at Ice expectantly.

"Elle Rollins," Ice said. "But not for transport. I will not take her to Sintaz only to imprison her in a dome she cannot easily leave, not after what she did for me. That is not a life I would condemn her to."

"Forget that last command. I need transport for four and a health report on Elle Rollins, gunshot wound—"

"In her side," Ice inserted.

"—in her side," Gary ordered through the handheld. The response he received was not in any language Ice understood. Gary handed the handheld back to Frost. "They are coming. You should be on alert."

"Why?" Snow looked around. "What did the ship say?"

"Mm, nothing," Gary mumbled, not looking directly at them. He pointed up an incline. "We should keep moving. No reason to dally."

"What is dally?" Frost whispered as he leaned closer to Ice.

"I think it is when they count items," Ice answered.

"Why would we count...?" Frost again looked around.

"That is tally," Snow interrupted his brothers. "I think dally is when a human goes to a private room and—"

"This way, this way," Gary insisted. For a smaller alien, he moved fast when he wanted to.

"I hear something," Frost said. "This sound is not like the others."

Ice had been thinking of Elle more than paying attention to what was going on around them. He tilted his head and nodded as he detected footsteps.

"Someone comes," Snow said.

All three brothers turned to look at Gary. He made a weak noise and said, "I told you not to dally."

"Is this a trap?" Ice demanded. He grabbed Gary by the arms and lifted him off the ground. "What did you do?"

"We adjusted the ground sensors after you were taken last time." Gary's legs kicked in the air. "I didn't want you to think we were incompetent after we missed there being a threat last time."

Air pressed down on them from above and Ice looked up as a ship passed. The running lights were off, and it was hard to see the craft except for how it blocked the moonlight and cast a shadow over the ground. Ice set Gary down and the alien ran after the ship.

"Go," Ice ordered his brothers. They ran after Gary. A soft glow of light indicated a ship door was opening to let them in.

A plank extended from the spaceship. It wasn't a large vessel, and not meant for long-range travel, but the main ship would be nearby.

"This way," a man bellowed.

Ice paused, letting his brothers go up the plank as he turned away from the ship to watch for trouble.

"You're not sacrificing yourself to save us this time," Snow said, reappearing next to him.

"Don't think we've forgotten that act of stupidity," Frost added. "You can bet we'll be having a discussion about that later."

His brothers grabbed his arms and pulled him up the plank. They entered the ship.

"*Ah.*"

The feminine sound was faint, but enough to make Ice inhale sharply in recognition.

The plank began to retract.

"I'm sorry, brothers, but I can't go back with you. I can't leave her." Ice grabbed hold of the entryway and launched his body forward, over the plank, so that he landed on the ground. He bent his knees, listening for Elle. The ship's door closed and clicked into place behind him.

Figures appeared in the moonlight, dark, shadowy men. He heard banging behind him as his brothers tried to get off the ship. He willed Galaxy Brides to take off. Now that he knew his brothers were safe and on their way home, he could concentrate on Elle.

He could pick her voice out of a chorus of millions. What was she doing out here?

The banging lessened, and the ship began pulling away from the surface.

When she didn't make another noise, he yelled, "Elle!"

"Ice, run," she screamed. "Run—"

The sound was abruptly cut short.

Ice *did* run. He went toward her voice. It didn't matter what happened to him as long as she was safe. He yelled as he charged into battle, using all the pent-up anger he felt toward the Milano Foundation.

"Don't shoot, I need the aliens whole," someone ordered. "Tasers only. You three, stop that ship from taking off. Do whatever you have to. Shoot it down, but don't let them get away!"

"Ice, get out of here!" Elle grunted and cried out in pain.

"Elle, where are you?" Ice tried to follow the sound of her voice. He threw his arm to the side, clotheslining someone who approached. He knocked the man to the ground. "Elle!"

"*Mmm-aaahh.*" Her scream was muffled.

"You want your girlfriend? Come and get her," the man in charge taunted. He recognized the scientist, Dr. Hanklen, who had done the tests on him.

Ice came to a stop as he entered a small clearing in the trees. The scientist stood beside Elle, who lay on the ground clutching her stomach. He held a gun trained on her.

"Let me help reunite the lovebirds." Luther reached down and grabbed Elle by the hair. He jerked her up. She flailed weakly as he forced her to stand. "There, that's better. Why don't you come over here and give her a kiss?"

Luther pressed his lips together in a mocking gesture.

Ice cringed. "You are not to my liking and you smell like cheese."

Luther scowled. He let go of Elle's hair. She stumbled but didn't fall. Dr. Hanklen pulled her arm and forced her next to him, pressing the gun into her side.

"He speaks English," Dr. Hanklen said to Elle. "You told us he didn't understand anything."

"Fuck it. Kick his ass, Ice," Elle yelled.

Ice wasn't sure why, but the doctor didn't stop

him from fighting Luther. The man charged, aiming his shoulder for Ice's stomach.

Ice braced himself for the blow, anchoring his feet as he leaned forward. He used the force of the man's strike to help him lift Luther's weight up and over. He flipped the human over his shoulder, jarring Luther's stomach before dropping him. When he turned, Luther was rolling over onto his hands and knees. Ice did as Elle had commanded and kicked him in the backside with the heel of his foot.

The man slid but did not fall to the ground. He rolled to the side before Ice could kick him again.

"Imagine what we'll be able to do with a specimen like this, what we'll learn from him," Dr. Hanklen said.

"You're a monster," Elle seethed.

"You're probably right," Dr. Hanklen agreed.

Luther swept his leg as he came out of the roll. He hit Ice in the back of the knees and sent him hard onto his back. The breath left his lungs in a rush and he gasped several times to get it back.

"Ice, get up!" Elle called.

He kicked his legs, pushing his body up from the ground so he landed on his feet. He glanced at

Elle. She leaned away from Dr. Hanklen, who didn't release her arm.

The fight became a fury of closed fist punches and open-handed palm thrusts. He heard the man's knuckles crack as he hit Ice's stomach. That is why one shouldn't fight with fists.

Stupid human.

He grunted in pain as a fist hit his jaw. In return, he shoved his palm hard into the man's chest, near his heart.

Luther's eyes widened as he grabbed his chest. He fell to his knees. Ice followed him down, hitting him in the face to make sure he stayed down.

Three fighters came from the woods. They surrounded Ice. Though they were smaller in size, their number would make it harder to defend against after the beating he'd just taken. Still, he lifted his hands, circling as he waited for the first to strike.

"Get him," Dr. Hanklen ordered.

Suddenly, a battle cry rang out from the trees —and he heard the charging feet of his brothers. They'd gotten off the ship to aid him.

"Go back," Ice ordered. "You can't be here."

"We're not leaving you to have all the fun," Snow dismissed.

Snow forced one of the three men to face him instead. Frost appeared and did the same with a second man. That left Ice with the third. The battle was over before it started. Snow took a few blows before locking his arm around the man's neck and riding him to the ground until he passed out. Frost hit his opponent hard that he fell and did not get back up.

Ice's man jumped back and ran into the forest.

The three brothers faced Dr. Hanklen.

"Is this Elle?" Snow asked.

"Nice." Frost grinned. "Are there more of her?"

"Stay back or I'll kill her," Dr. Hanklen warned, jamming the barrel into her so hard she cried out in pain.

"Kill her and we kill you," Snow said. "Slowly."

"Shoot one of us and we kill you," Frost added.

"I think you can see how this is going to go," Ice said.

Dr. Hanklen eyed each of them in turn. "This isn't over."

He released Elle, shoving her at Ice before slowly backing away. She fell weakly against him and couldn't support her own weight. He lifted her into his arms. His brothers instantly formed a shield around her as they faced the doctor. Ice knew his brothers would do everything they could to protect his woman.

Hanklen backed away, his gun pointing at them. Snow and Frost took a step back, prompting Ice to carry Elle into the trees.

Suddenly, Hanklen turned and dove behind an uprooted tree.

"Go," Snow ordered.

Ice didn't have to be told again. He carried Elle as Frost darted ahead to lead the way back to the ship. It had moved locations, but they found it hidden in the shadows of a small cliff.

Frost banged on the metal. Seconds later, the door opened. Ice glanced behind them to make sure they weren't being followed. Snow stood between them and the trees to offer protection.

"Get her inside." Frost tugged Ice's arm, prompting him to go first.

Ice ducked into the spaceship. The metal holding area wasn't pretty, but it had seats. He set Elle on the largest one and strapped her in. The door closed, and they heard the rumble of an engine. Ice sat next to her. Her head dropped but her eyes were open.

Holding her hand as they took off, he didn't take his gaze from hers.

"You came back for me," she whispered, a ghost of a smile on her face.

"I could not leave you," Ice said.

"You're his woman," Snow stated loudly from his chair.

The ship shifted, and he felt the pressure of takeoff.

"He loves you," Frost added. "We saw it."

"I take it these are your brothers." Elle's smile fell a little and her eyes closed as the pressure increased. She seemed to struggle with holding up her head.

He saw the hint of blood on her shirt, from where she'd been shot. As soon as they reached space, he would make sure she was put into a medical booth and healed. He remembered seeing one on the ship.

"They are not wrong." Ice held her hand tighter. "I do love you, Elle. I can't leave you."

"I'll go," Elle said, not looking at him. "Wherever you want to be, I'll go too. I love you, Ice.

When I thought I'd lost you forever, I couldn't bear the pain of it."

"Try to stay awake, Elle." He could only hold her hand but it was enough. He felt her warmth, detected the beat of her heart in her wrist. "I'll take care of you. I promise. Just hold on a little longer."

18

One week later...

ELLE SAT ON HER PARENTS' PORCH surrounded by the beauty of Voyageurs National Park. Sunset in Northern Minnesota fascinated Ice and his brothers, and they all three stood on the lawn gazing at the sky. No one would look for her here. The Milano Foundation would be hunting for Ellen Sharp who'd grown up in Long Island and had no living relatives. The foundation didn't know about this place. No one did. She could only hope the foundation took the lies on her application at face value and didn't question her identity to the point they discovered the falsehoods.

That didn't mean the threat wasn't still there. The Milano Foundation would still want to capture the Sintazians. They would have to be vigilant. If trouble came, it was just a small hop into Canada. She knew the terrain, and they'd be able to walk across the border. It would buy them time to disappear. The envelope of cash that Ice gave her was hidden in the guest house for such a day.

She pulled the blankets tighter around her body to fight off the chilly weather. By the end of the month, snow would be falling, and it wouldn't stop until late April or May. It wasn't Sintazian temperatures, but she felt this was the best compromise she could manage.

They were safe. They had a home. Yes, explaining the whole alien thing to her parents had been tricky, but Elle thought they were coming around. Her parents insisted they stay, regardless of the strangeness of her guests. She knew her father would like Ice when he got to know him. How could he not? He might be an alien from outer space, but Ice was the most honorable man she'd ever known.

The blue had started coming back to their complexions. All except Frost, who could not take the medicine needed to get rid of his true coloring. Here, in the isolation of the national park, they didn't need to hide who they were. Locals tended to keep to themselves when it came to strangers but were always ready to help out a friend. She hoped that, in time, those who came to meet her new family would be understanding and offer them the same courtesies they would any other neighbor.

"We do not have skies like this on my planet." Ice joined her on the porch. He sat beside her on a bench and held her against him. He rubbed his hand against her arm as if to warm her. "Is there any pain today?"

"Please stop worrying. I promise I'm fine. Whatever those Galaxy Brides aliens did with their magic machine worked. It's like I was never shot." She tapped her side. The memory of the pain was still there, but the skin was healed. "I wish Earth would get its shit together. And maybe the aliens would share that technology with us and we could end world suffering."

"When the time is right, the reptilians will make contact." Ice kept rubbing her arm. "Are you very cold?"

"It's not bad tonight," she answered.

"You feel cold to me."

"Stop fussing. I'm fine." She laid her head against his shoulder.

"No. I think I should warm you."

Elle got his meaning and laughed as she lifted her head to look at him. "Mm, maybe you're right. I do feel a sudden chill coming on. I don't think this blanket will be enough."

"Elle." Frost approached, stopping them from leaving the porch. "I have made up my mind. I do not wish to go back when Galaxy Brides comes to check on us in four months. I would like to stay here. Will you help me find a place? And a woman? I would like a woman."

"I would like a woman too." Snow joined them. "And a place. But mostly a woman."

"I would love for you to stay on Earth." Elle knew that would make Ice very happy. "The place, I can definitely help with. As for the women..." She started to deny them, but seeing the hope in their expressions, she said, "I'll have to see what I can do."

Ice grinned as he stood. "Stop talking. I am going to warm my woman now."

Elle coughed in surprise at his blunt state-ment. She was not used to talking about sex so openly. However, between the brothers, there didn't seem to be many secrets. In fact, when she was in the medical booth, Ice had apparently told them all about her and their experiences together. He had not left out any of the details. When she woke in the medical booth, they begin asking her strange questions about sexual positions, and if human women preferred to mate in the backs of trucks or in the cold.

"I would like to be more than your woman, Ice." She wrapped her arms around his neck.

"I do not understand, my love."

"I want to be your wife. I want to be yours forever. Ask me to marry you." She touched his cheek.

"But aren't we married?" Ice frowned and looked at his brothers for confirmation.

"You have spoken words of love," Frost said.

"You have come together for sex," Snow added.

"Many times," Ice answered.

Elle hid her grimace. She would have to talk to him about his openness. It wouldn't do for him to talk about sex in front of their neighbors or, God forbid, her parents.

"You have chosen to be with each other."

Frost glanced at Snow, and they both furrowed their brows in thought. "What else is there?"

"See, you are my wife." Ice kissed her as if sealing the statement. "It is already done."

"For the record, that's not how we do things around here. And I'm going to let *you* be the one who tells my mother she doesn't get to plan a big wedding for her only daughter." Elle laughed.

"Can I do it later?" he whispered, glancing toward the guesthouse where he stayed with his brothers.

"Race ya." Elle let go of him and began to run across the yard. She giggled as Ice easily overtook her and swept her over his shoulder with barely breaking his stride.

The End

Galaxy Alien Mail Order Brides Series

Spark

Flame

Blaze

Ice

Frost

Snow

If you enjoyed the Galaxy Alien Mail Order Brides by Michelle M. Pillow, you'll love:

Determined Prince

Captured by a Dragon-Shifter Series

Dragon-shifter Prince Kyran has studied the Earth people and is ready to assimilate. Female shifters are all but going extinct on his planet of Quril-ixen, and his people are desperate for mates—so much so they're taking matters into their own hands. What better place to capture a woman than Earth? After all, dragon-shifters had come from there centuries ago. Surely a human female would be honored to be selected by one as fine and fierce as himself?

While on Earth, Kyran stumbles upon the most beautiful woman he's ever imagined, singing something the natives call rock 'n' roll. His blood simmers and he knows Eve is the one for him. But taming this feisty female is going to take much more than his training prepared him for.

CHAPTER ONE EXCERPT

Prince Kyran adjusted the bandana around his neck as he peered deeper into the dark cave hidden within the mountain. At least, he was fairly sure the thing around his neck was called a bandana. Or was it a handkerchief? It was hard to remember all the human words. Technically, his people still spoke a dialect of an Earth language, but so much had changed in the centuries since they'd left the planet, that many new words and customs had to be learned.

"My name is Kyran. You look like an honorable woman," he whispered, practicing what he would say to any prospective mate. "I have a home with my parents and my brother. There we will live and you will be part of our family. Would you like to give me many children?"

Behind him, the mountain valley air was sweet, a blend of grasses and tiny blue flowers. It mixed with the almost acidic smell of porous black rocks now surrounding him. It wasn't the darkness that caused the tiny jolt of apprehension in his stomach. His shifter eyes could easily cut through the shadows. It was what awaited him beyond the dark stone walls—marriage.

Kyran smiled thoughtfully to himself, perhaps simple was best. "Come to my home planet and I will make you my princess."

The Draig, Kyran's people, were a race of dragon-shifters. Long ago, they'd escaped Earth, using a portal to come to a place where they could live out in the open, free of persecution. The Var, friends of the Draig people, had come with them. Vars were cat-shifters and had just as much reason to leave the old world. Only by working together had the two races managed to make a clean start. It was an alliance so strong that Kyran couldn't imagine it ever changing.

Perhaps he should try poetic. "You will like my planet. Qurilixen is a wondrous place bathed in almost constant daylight. In the valley near the borderlands, there is a forest of oversized trees—so big that from a distance the taller ones look like your castle homes on Earth. Here we will join and become one."

Though he'd never actually been to Earth himself, Kyran had seen pictures of the old palaces in the royal library, and they were very much like the castle he and his family lived in. Only some of the elders could actually remember making the trip across, and they had been little help as to what to expect. A few scouts had been through the portal to study modern Earth and to make sure the trip would be safe. They spoke of tall square castles and loud noises.

"This will be easy," he told himself in determination. "Earth has many women. Finding one will not be hard. I have studied the transmissions. I am ready for this assimilation into Earth culture. I am a fierce dragon and will make a fine husband. A woman would be lucky to have me. I will find a princess." Fear tried to work its way into his brain, but he pushed it aside. He had to stay determined. This had to work—not only for him, but for his people.

Luckily, Earth had advanced to a state that

humans aired transmissions. They called it television, and once the shifters had learned to capture those waves, they'd been able to study the new Earth culture to practice blending in.

"How-ow-dee-ee," he sounded out slowly, trying to mimic the wavy intonation of the customary greeting. He liked the cowmen. They appeared to be a tough breed of humans who spent much time outdoors riding funny looking ceffyls around open fields.

Blending was better than the royals' original plan of sneaking through the portal and kidnapping human women like the barbaric tribes written about in old scrolls. At least this way, they could get a good look at the females before they snatched them. To some, the idea seemed extreme —bringing women through the portal in order to marry them. It had taken decades before enough of the elders had finally agreed to the plan. Unfortunately, the Draig and Var no longer had a choice. If they didn't find compatible mates soon, their kind would die out in a generation. The few alien species who had made contact were not mating material for a number of reasons—incompatible biology, conflicting customs, no desire to live onworld.

For some reason, female shifters were no longer being born. The males thrived, growing stronger, living much longer than before. Couples had even been encouraged to have more babies to up the odds. Nothing worked. Now they had a large generation of men with little hope of marriage. Their best scholars were working on the problem, but until a solution was found, for the sake of their survival, they needed to find brides.

Historical documents indicated humans were reproductively compatible. This portal was their best hope, a way for the men of their planet to have a chance at happiness.

Their ancestors had caved in the portal when they'd first arrived on Qurilixen. Apparently, they'd thought no one would ever want to go back and wished to keep humans from following. Only after years of digging had the Draig unearthed it. Prince Kyran would be one of the first four grooms to go through. It was his duty to show the people this plan would work.

Many elders weren't happy with the plan to find mates this way, for they still carried the emotional scars from the old days. Human religions had changed, and with their new beliefs had come the idea that all shifters had made pacts with some person named Demon. If there were signed treaties with this Demon, any records had been lost.

Some shifters hoped time had changed the humans. Because of the controversy, the four princes had volunteered to go first and prove this could work. Prince Kyran and his younger brother, Prince Finn of the Draig, would join Princes Ivar and Rafe of the Var. It wasn't decreed which of them would come back with a bride, only that they had to start looking.

"Ready?" Finn asked, coming from behind Kyran carrying a torch. He glanced over Kyran's outfit and smirked.

"What?" Kyran looked down. He looked exactly like a cowman with boots, a hat and tight pants. Actually, he'd chosen the style of dress for the tight pants. What better way to show off one of his finer assets? "It's better than what you picked."

Finn grinned. He was dressed as a great warrior. "We shall see who turns the most heads, brother."

Hearing a noise, both dragon-shifters turned. Prince Ivar's green gaze glinted from the darkened shadows. When he stepped forward into the torchlight, he wore the native clothing of the cat-shifters. Fitted black pants pulled low across the hips, showing off a fair amount of stomach. The matching black shirt was laced down the center front, revealing a strip of his chest. Kyran quirked a brow.

Ivar waved a hand in dismissal. "The tailor brought me a gown and said I was to go to this accursed planet in it. I refused. I much rather receive stares than blend in as a woman—royal Earth custom or not. What is a *draqueen* anyway? It sounds like your ancestors, not mine, dragons."

Kyran shared a look with his brother. Finn shrugged. He didn't know either.

"Where's Rafe?" Kyran asked. "The portal's about to open."

"Here!" Prince Rafe called. His footfall sounded over the cave as he jogged forward. His white pants belled wide at the bottom, matching the white long-sleeved shirt. Rafe glanced at his brother's non-attire and said distractedly, "Sorry."

The more serious Ivar grunted. "You lost track of time before *this*?"

"I felt like someone was following me. I doubled back to the borderlands before return-ing," Rafe said. Then defensively, he added to

Ivar, "You think I'm paranoid, but I'm telling you, not every Var wants to see us marry humans. Arguments are still being made that taking humans will dilute shifter blood and cause us to lose our natural abilities. They would rather we take to the stars and meet other humanoid species or wait for the gods to bless us."

"It is not their place to question a Var royal decree," Ivar stated to his brother. "The elder council had their say. This will be."

"Shall we?" Kyran wanted to stop the two cat-shifter brothers before they began yelling. Moving to walk deeper into the cave, he glanced over his shoulder to see if the others followed.

"I don't know why you're so eager to meet your destiny, Kyran," Finn said.

"Aren't you?" Rafe asked. "I can't wait to find a bride to share my bed. The women ships don't come often enough for my taste."

"I've told you to stay away from those ships. You do not know what diseases the alien travelers carry in their profession," Ivar said.

"I only watch them dance," Rafe defended. He let fur sprout over his nose as he made a face at his brother's back. Finn hid his laugh.

"What if you get a shrew?" Ivar sounded

reasonable, like always.

"So long as she's shrewing in my bed, I don't care." Rafe winked.

Ivar grunted by way of an answer.

Kyran knew Rafe loved nothing more than to aggravate his stoic brother. "Come. The time is soon. Remember, only one is to find a bride this time. They want us to take it slowly."

"And I elect Kyran." Finn laughed, slapping his older brother's shoulder so hard Kyran stumbled. "This was his idea."

"Agreed," Rafe said quickly, not breaking stride.

Kyran opened his mouth as he righted himself, but Ivar had said, "Agreed," before he could get a word in. The three princes laughed. Kyran took a deep breath. He knew his duty, and if he must go first to ensure the future of his people, so be it.

"Ach! Come on then. Now is as good as later." Kyran forced a chuckle, not wanting to admit he was nervous. "So help me, when I'm finished you all had better go next. I'll not be the only prince settled."

MichellePillow.com

ABOUT THE AUTHOR

New York Times & *USA TODAY* Bestselling Author

Michelle loves to travel and try new things, whether it's a paranormal investigation of an old Vaudeville Theatre or climbing Mayan temples in Belize. She believes life is an adventure fueled by copious amounts of coffee.

Newly relocated to the American South, Michelle is involved in various film and documentary projects with her talented director husband. She is mom to a fantastic artist. And she's managed by a dog and cat who make sure she's meeting her deadlines.

For the most part she can be found wearing pajama pants and working in her office. There may or may not be dancing. It's all part of the creative process.

Come say hello! Michelle loves talking with readers on social media!

www.MichellePillow.com

facebook.com/AuthorMichellePillow

twitter.com/michellepillow

instagram.com/michellempillow

bookbub.com/authors/michelle-m-pillow

goodreads.com/Michelle_Pillow

amazon.com/author/michellepillow

youtube.com/michellepillow

pinterest.com/michellepillow

Free Reading Guides

Download free reading guides in MOBI or EPUB formats from MichellePillow.com.

COMPLIMENTARY EXCERPTS

TRY BEFORE YOU BUY!

Space Lords: His Frost Maiden
by Michelle M. Pillow

Empath and space pirate, Evan Cormier is obsessed with decoding an ominous premonition about his future. When a fellow crewman angered a spirit, the vengeful Zhang An took her wrath out on everyone in the vicinity. Evan just happened to be one of them. He's now facing a future in which he'll be forever alone.

Lady Josselyn of the House of Craven has been betrayed. With her home world on a Florencian moon under attack and her family dead, she finds herself at the mercy of the one who deceived them. There is only one thing left to do—die with honor. But before she can join her family in the afterlife, she must first avenge all that she held dear. Falling in love with a pirate was never in the plan. Evan and his thieving crewmates might have delayed her fate, but they can't stop destiny.

His Frost Maiden Excerpt

Craven Estates, Earth Settlement, Florencia's Fifth Moon

"Lift her," the General ordered, his shiny boots walking away from her, taking her reflection with it.

Two men hauled her to her feet, holding her up by her arms. Josselyn suppressed a cry as they jerked her dislocated shoulder. She couldn't see their faces, didn't need to. Her body hurt so badly she couldn't tell where the pain was coming from anymore.

The one who'd betrayed them stood before her. General Jack Stephans. He'd deceived her family and the fifth moon settlement. He'd traded them in for money and power. Josselyn lifted her gaze briefly to the hard depths of the steel green eyes before her. She wanted to kick, to give one last good blow, to go down fighting, but she couldn't raise her limbs.

"Poor little Josselyn, so heartbreaking," the General grabbed her chin and swiped beneath her eye. He looked young, was in fact very young for his position, only a few years older than her six and twenty. And yet they all knew so much more of fighting than anyone their age should, than anyone ever should.

"We gave you a home," she whispered. "How could you do this? How could you join them?"

"You gave me a place in your stables," he spat, his grip tightening on her chin, bruisingly so. "Not a place at your table. Not a place by your side. Not equal. They gave me a rank, a title. They give me respect. They give me a place in this world."

"Jack," she said, her voice softening for the orphan boy they'd found over twenty years ago. If she begged him, maybe fate could be turned around; maybe this day could be erased. Fate had spit them out in a whirlwind of chance and deceit. Maybe all that had happened wasn't his fault. Maybe it wasn't hers. None of it mattered. None of it changed the fact that he had taken everything she held dear, everyone, and now he was robbing her of her family home. Her tone hardened and she closed her eyes. "General."

"Look at me, Josselyn," he said. His tone caught even as his grip on her face tightened until his fingers pressed the inside of her cheeks against her teeth. "You're so cold. Even now, your face is composed. Is one, lonely tear all the passion you can muster?"

"I am Lady Josselyn of the House of Craven." Her eyes opened slowly, focusing on the shiny white of his uniform. It gleamed with the orange glow coming from the fireplace. The material looked odd in the drabber earth tones many on the fifth moon wore. Theirs was a world based on Medieval Earth. Each moon in the Florencian system was different, each settlement patterned off a singular time in the human past, times that history had almost forgotten. But the principals of the ancestors who'd established the colonies no longer applied. Times were different now. What had started as preservation of history had turned into reality, into laws and a way of life they all believed in as generation after generation was raised into the worlds of the Florencian moons.

The General shook her by the face until finally she forced her eyes to meet his. He looked angry, hurt, wildly hopeful. "I can save you. I can say you had nothing to do with the treachery of your family. No one wants to kill a woman of noble blood. The line of Craven doesn't have to die. I will take your name; the name denied me by your father."

Was he serious? She knew he'd asked her father for her hand in marriage. In fact, she'd dismissed the proposal with the full knowledge he only asked because he wanted power. Did he think she could love him now? Want him? Take him into her bed?

He must have read the answer on her face because his own expression hardened. She knew Jack. He wouldn't ask again.

"I suppose not," he said, almost sad. "Even if you agreed, I could never trust you not to take a blade to my back. Not after today." He sighed heavily. "Not after this."

"Ago," she whispered, even her voice beginning to fail in its strength, "pugna quod int-"

"Quiet your tongue! This house is mine. Mine." He let go of her chin and her head drooped. "And you can die knowing that I have taken more than what you all refused to give me in life."

"A place at our table," Josselyn said, her tone softer still, the will to live leaving her. Her heart called out to her ancestors, to her dead family, begging them to come and get her.

"My table," he answered, stepping away. The General lifted a gun, pointing it at her head. She heard the telltale click of metal on metal. The weapon was not one found on the fifth moon. They fought with swords and axes, like the old medieval ways. Though technology was available, not using it was a point of honor. He must have brought the weapon from another moon. Perhaps the Victorians? The Elizabethans? It appeared to be too old to be from much later in time.

"Do it, Jack." She didn't look at him as she waited for the final discharge of the gun, the loud bang before the end. When it didn't come, she repeated, the words a mere mouthing of her lips, "Do it."

"Speed you to a quick end, Josselyn Craven," Jack whispered. "You all brought this on yourselves."

www.MichellePillow.com

Space Lords Series

His Frost Maiden
His Fire Maiden
His Metal Maiden
His Earth Maiden
His Woodland Maiden

Fan of Michelle M. Pillow?

Want to join an awesome group of readers?
www.facebook.com/groups/MichellePillowFanClub

9 781625 012173